Life With LEMON
Tales and Legends

Neil Mohan Sehgal

INDIA · SINGAPORE · MALAYSIA

I want to express my gratitude to my elder sister, Mauly, and my wife, Meenakshi. Without them, this book wouldn't be possible. Meenakshi is always my first reader and critic, encouraging me to write more. And my sister, who never refuses to get me any book I want to read, no questions asked.

Lastly, I want to dedicate this book to my child, who was born on January 28, 2024 (Avyukt). I hope he will find it relevant and connect with it as he grows up.

As you read through, you'll be drawn into vibrant settings and diverse characters, with each story and poem leaving a lasting impression.

Prologue

"Life with Lemon-tales and Legends" is a captivating collection of short stories and poems that lets readers enjoy the different experiences people go through. Each story and poem is like a small piece, giving a peek into both ordinary and special moments.

The tales in *"Life with Lemon-tales and Legends"* feel like cherished memories, touching on themes of connection, discovery, and surprises. The author skillfully combines realism, whimsy, and reflection of life in stories to take readers on a journey through the pages. The author's ability to capture the essence of diverse settings and characters showcases a deep understanding of the human condition.

The stories and poems, each a carefully crafted snapshot, invite readers to pause, ponder, and

appreciate the beauty found in the simple and extraordinary moments of life.

For the Love of the books

This Fine Morning, I woke up, made my morning tea and went on with a book in my hand, after reading a page or two I feel like romanticising the book and kissed it... .ahhhh "What a beautiful day to be alive and reading... "

- Neil

Contents

Contents

Stories

1

The Unborn Oracle

In the quaint town where time seemed to move at a leisurely pace, our life unfolded gently through daily routine. It was a day like any other, filled with the ordinary yet treasured moments that we had grown accustomed to in our small haven.

The air in our house filled with joy and expectation. My wife, with a glow that only expectant mothers possess, was six months into her pregnancy. Our first child, a yet-to-be-born entity, had become a central character in our daily lives. It seemed that this tiny soul had already embraced the world's rhythms, engaging in a daily ballet of kicks, boxing, and reactions to the familiar voices that surrounded it.

In this particular year, a dormant passion from my childhood rekindled its flame. The game of cricket, a beloved pursuit from my younger days, became a source of renewed enthusiasm. After the day's toils, I found solace and joy in those extra moments that I could dedicate to the sport. As the sun dipped below the horizon, and we were done with our daily scheduled work, I would engage in a unique ritual – conversing with the life growing within my wife's womb.

The unborn child responded to our voices, his movements akin to a secret language only we could decipher. It was during one such evening, with the golden hues of the setting sun casting a warm glow, that a whimsical idea crossed my mind. What if, I pondered, I could seek insights into my recent cricket performances from the yet-to-be-born child within?

Excitedly, I shared this playful thought with my wife. As we laughed about the absurdity of the idea, the baby seemed to join the conversation, expressing its own opinion through a swift kick. Amused by this unexpected participation, we revelled in the enchantment of the moment. My wife, with a playful twinkle in her eye, placed her hand over her belly and asked, "How will papa perform in the coming match?"

The first query hung in the air without a response, but when she mischievously suggested, "Will papa score a zero?" – the baby, almost on cue, reacted with a lively kick in the movement. Laughter filled the room, and we drifted into sleep, the memory of this light-hearted banter became part of our dream story.

As the day unfolded, I found myself wearing the whites once again to open the innings for my team. Determined to break the pattern of dull performances,

I approached the crease with a resolve that mirrored the intensity of the summer sun.

The opposing bowler, a formidable adversary, embarked on his run-up. In my mind, I was already strategising the perfect defence against the impending delivery. However, fate has a way of surprising even the most prepared minds. The ball, instead of obeying my mental commands, took an unexpected edge off my bat, sailing into the keeper's gloves. I was dismissed for a golden duck, my disappointment noticeable in the silence that settled over the field.

Walking back to the team dugout, I couldn't shake off the echo of the unborn child's playful prediction. It seemed as if the baby, in its mysterious wisdom, had foreseen the cricketing twist of fate. The absurd thought lingered in my mind – could our child be more than just a playful kicker in the womb? Was there a touch of the divine, a glimpse into the mystical world of fate and fortune?

The sun dipped below the horizon, casting long shadows on the cricket field. In that moment of introspection, a wry smile tugged at my lips. Perhaps, just perhaps, our child will be destined for a life as a fortune-teller, a self-proclaimed or an oracle. The absurdity of the idea brought a broader smile to my lips, even in the face of my bad cricketing performance.

2

Tragic Festival Journey

Laxmi's summer sojourn in the quaint village of Uttarakhand began with a sense of tranquillity that enveloped her grandparents' home. Surrounded by the majestic beauty of the mountains and dense forests, she found herself in a world far removed from the hustle and bustle of city life. However, the stillness of the surroundings couldn't dispel the quiet loneliness that settled within her.

In this secluded haven, Laxmi discovered her sole companion—a canine confidant named Bhura. His fur, a medley of earthy tones, matched the rustic charm of the village. Bhura had claimed the porch of her grandparents' house as his domain, and from there, he would embark on explorations of the winding trails and thick woods with Laxmi.

Their days unfolded in a series of adventures through the dense forests, along the gushing river, and beneath the towering mountains. Bhura, with his perky ears and wagging tail, became Laxmi's silent confidant.

Amidst the whispering trees and rustling leaves, Laxmi found solace in sharing her dreams, secrets, and fears with her four-legged friend.

The village, though dotted with the laughter of children in neighbouring houses, failed to captivate Laxmi's interest. Her favourite pastime became exploring the new and old trails, with Bhura trotting alongside her, his keen senses attuned to the nuances of the natural world. Their bond deepened with each passing day, an unspoken connection that transcended the boundaries of human and canine.

Laxmi's grandparents, affectionately known as Dada and Dadi, were the living embodiments of the village's history.

Dada, with his snow-white beard and deeply etched laugh lines, was a repository of traditional tales and ancestral wisdom. His eyes, though weathered by time, sparkled with the twinkle of mischief that often revealed itself in his impromptu storytelling sessions. The creaky rocking chair on the porch, under the shade of a gnarled old tree, was his throne from which he regaled anyone willing to lend an ear.

Dadi, a lively woman with a perpetual twinkle in her eye, was the heart of the household. She was the keeper of family recipes, the matriarch performing the daily rhythm of life. Her mornings began with the clanging of pots and pans, creating an aromatic symphony that wafted through the house. Dadi's kitchen was a haven of flavours, where generations-old recipes whispered secrets of love and sustenance.

One peculiar trait of Dadi, however, was her penchant for forgetting names. It became a source of light-hearted banter in the village, as Dadi, with her infectious laughter, would attempt to recall the names of the neighbours, the children, and even her cattle. Each morning, she'd embark on a mission to greet everyone by name, armed with a mental checklist that often led to amusing encounters.

On one such occasion, Laxmi observed Dadi's morning routine unfold with comedic charm. As Dadi bustled about the kitchen, preparing a feast for the day, the door creaked open, and our neighbour, Mr. Sharma, stepped in.

"Good morning, Dadi! How are you today?" Mr. Sharma greeted her with a warm smile.

Dadi, engrossed in her culinary symphony, turned around, her eyes squinting in thought. "Ah, good morning, my dear friend! How is... um, what's your name again?" she quizzically inquired.

Mr. Sharma chuckled, accustomed to this routine. "It's Sharma, Dadi. Mr. Sharma."

Dadi's face lit up with recognition. "Ah, yes, yes! Sharma! How could I forget? Come, have some chai, Sharma-ji!"

Laxmi, observing the exchange, giggled in the corner.

This daily ritual had become a source of village amusement, a character trait that only added to Dadi's charm. As the days unfolded, Laxmi found herself entwined in the tapestry of village life, each thread woven with the nuances of tradition and the vibrant colours of community.

One morning, Dadi delivered news of a local festival set to unfold in a nearby town. An opportunity to immerse herself in the rich cultural tapestry of the region presented itself, Laxmi's initial hesitation gave way to curiosity. Dadi, sensing the stirrings of adventure in her granddaughter's heart, encouraged her to partake in the festivities.

Dadi told Laxmi, "Traditions are the threads that weave the fabric of our culture, Laxmi. Embrace them, for they hold the stories of our people."

"And who knows when you'll return next to experience this again?"

With a tentative nod, Laxmi agreed to attend the festival, her mind already buzzing with thoughts of vibrant colours, lively music, and the joyous dance that awaited her.

The following day, as Laxmi and Bhura explored a nearby trail, a burst of colour and melody disrupted their tranquil ambience. A procession of local villagers comprising seasoned musicians, their melodies echoed through the hills, infusing life into every celebration. 'Cholias,' named after the vibrant Choliya dance form that accompanied their music, were an integral part of the village's cultural identity. Adorned in traditional attire, singing and dancing, passed them. Laxmi's eyes lit up at the spectacle, and she turned to Bhura with an excited gleam.

"What do you say, Bhura? Shall we join the festivities?" she asked, a sparkle in her eyes.

Bhura, ever the perceptive companion, responded with an exuberant nod and a playful whinny. The decision was made. Laxmi and Bhura would attend the festival in the evening, ready to immerse themselves in the cultural revelry.

As the sun dipped below the horizon, casting a warm glow over the village, they made their way to the town. The festival was a riot of colours, a kaleidoscope of traditional dances, rhythmic music, and the jubilant chatter of the crowd. Laxmi and Bhura found themselves at the heart of the celebration, dancing to the infectious beats with unbridled joy.

Yet, in the midst of the festivities, shadows lurked. A group of revellers, fuelled by the intoxicating spirits of the festival, stumbled upon Laxmi and Bhura. Oblivious to the sanctity of the occasion, they found amusement in sharing their liquor with the dog. Pouring the concoction into a bowl with chicken bones, they offered it to Bhura.

The consequences unfolded swiftly. Bhura, unaware of the serious and immediate danger he faced, lapped up the poisoned mixture with innocent enthusiasm. Laxmi, initially caught up in the celebration, soon sensed that something was amiss. Bhura's playful demeanour morphed into confusion and distress, his once-bright eyes clouded with pain.

Panicked, Laxmi attempted to look up the cause of Bhura's sudden anguish. The revellers, revelling in their own mirth, revealed the cruel prank they had played on the dog. The liquor, intended for human consumption, wreaked havoc on Bhura's delicate system. The festival's joyful cacophony faded into the background as Laxmi, faced with a dire situation, sought help in the chaotic sea of celebration.

Frantic and desperate, Laxmi carried Bhura in her arms, racing against time to reach their village. The sun had long set, shrouding the landscape in darkness as they navigated the familiar trails now fraught with urgency. The festival's echoes faded into the distance as Laxmi's singular focus became clear: to save Bhura.

Arriving at their house, Laxmi cradled Bhura, his strength waning with each passing moment. The festive cheers that once filled the air now gave way to a heavy silence. Bhura, once filled with energy and excitement, lay limp in Laxmi's arms, his laboured breaths echoing the severity of the situation.

In the dim light of their village home, Bhura's once-bright eyes gradually closed. Laxmi clung to him, whispering words of love and sorrow as her dear friend took his final breath. The tragedy unfolded in the quiet confines of the house, a stark contrast to the celebratory fervour that had drawn them to the festival.

The poignant tale of Laxmi and Bhura serves as a haunting reminder of the consequences of thoughtless actions and the fragility of the bond between humans and animals. In the wake of this heart-wrenching experience, Laxmi's grief was not only for the loss of her beloved companion but also for the stark revelation of human callousness amidst the backdrop of a festive celebration. The incident prompted reflections on empathy, compassion, and the responsibility we bear in our interactions with the creatures that share our world.

As Laxmi navigated the ebb and flow of emotions, the village, once a haven of solitude, became a poignant backdrop to her healing journey. The familiar trails, once traversed with Bhura's bounding steps, now echoed with the melancholy of memories. The festivals, once a source of communal joy, carried a bittersweet resonance, a reminder of the night that altered the course of Laxmi's summer holidays.

3

Dadi ji's House Nightmare

Ramnagar, a small picturesque town nestled in the Kumaon region of Uttarakhand, is my birthplace. This charming town is situated on the banks of the Kosi River, with the spectacular backdrop of the majestic Himalayan range. Known for its natural beauty, wildlife, and cultural richness, this small town serves as a gateway to one of India's oldest national parks (Jim Corbett) and a haven for wildlife enthusiasts.

Surrounded by dense forest, rolling hills, and the soothing sound of the Kosi River flowing through the town, every person in town is a tale in itself.

Our house, located in one of the oldest buildings in the town with walls made from river stone, has stood tall for more than 100 years. If I were to give you an outlook of the house, it's a duplex of those times.

Since my early childhood years, I have always been captivated by the enchanting beauty of my hometown until one day our elders decided to split up and move to the big city for the betterment of everybody's future.

The visits to the old house were very frequent at first, but after a point, they became more occasional or seasonal.

With time, I also navigated from childhood to adolescence with a newfound sense of maturity and accomplishment, leaving behind a majestic realm of forest, mountains, and enigmatic people's tales.

It was the year of my high school, and for a change, our family decided to take a break and visit our grandfather's house in Ramnagar to meet our uncle and aunt in the summer holidays.

Travelling always evokes strange nostalgic feelings within me and leads me to unexplored spaces in my head, thoughts that are left behind buried with the never -ending hustles, thoughts which I have kept securely in the remotest corner of my mind that one day I will make them alive, I will make them real.

With all these thoughts of joy, sorrow, and the unknown, we reached Ramnagar, and in no time, we were all sitting in a small cosy room, laughing, hugging, enjoying tea, and taking stock of what all we missed living in the city. As we finished our supper, everybody dispersed to their respective rooms for sleep.

The day went by, and moonlight cast long shadows across the courtyard. As nights got deeper, it seemed eerily silent.

Unable to sleep, fear of childhood memories started recurring in my mind of going alone to the lonely parts of the house.

Somewhere around midnight, a sudden urgency jolted me awake. I realised it was nature's call. I looked up at the clock; it was 2 am. A chill went through my body thinking of going alone in the night across the hall to the bathroom. I slowly called my cousin sleeping next to me, but all I could get back was a long, dark snore. I realised there was no alternative but to get up and release the pressure. In the quiet of the night, I got out of my bed and started walking across the hall. The house was all silent, and I got this feeling that someone's there, just behind me. The darkness, thick and heavy, made everything seem scarier, like there's something hiding in the shadows.

As I walked through the house, I started hearing strange sounds – the floor creaked, and it was like the house was whispering secrets I couldn't quite catch. The air felt tight, like there was a spooky presence lingering around. My heart started beating faster, matching the creepy feeling that crept up on me. I just wanted to quickly finish my business and get back to bed as soon as possible.

With every step I took, my own heartbeat echoed loudly, as if it was telling me to hurry up and get away from whatever might be hiding in the dark.

Every corner looked like it was hiding something, and my mind started playing tricks on me, making me see scary shadows that weren't really there. It was like the house was full of secrets, and I was trapped in my own fear.

Moving from a dimly lit room to the hall, I felt a cold shiver down my spine, like someone had just touched me. The whole atmosphere became heavy, and it was as if the walls themselves were closing in on me, making me feel trapped in a nightmare.

In this lonely moment, with my imagination running faster and faster, I couldn't tell what was real and what was just in my head. The fear of something jumping out from the dark became so real, turning a simple walk through the house into a scary journey. As I reached the bathroom, I was struck with surprise – the bathroom door was locked, and with each passing second, the pressure became unbearable.

Forced to find an alternative, I, against my wish, decided to descend into the basement. The creaking stairs seemed to groan in protest as I made my way down. The air down there felt heavy, laden with secrets and forgotten tales. The dimly lit environment barely illuminated the path, and the horror above once again chased me downstairs.

As I traversed through the shadowy hallway in the basement, my eyes caught a glimpse of an unexpected presence – my grandmother's imposing portrait, looming in the darkness. I froze in my tracks, my heart pounding in my chest. I hadn't known it was there, and its sudden appearance unsettled me. The stern gaze of the old woman in the painting seemed to follow me as I continued my desperate journey to the bathroom.

In haste, I finished my business and started making my way back. However, what awaited me turned that night into a nightmare. In the glow of the dim light, a lean figure lay on the sofa – a frail, old woman draped in a white sari. Panic seized me, and I couldn't comprehend what I was seeing. My mind played tricks on me, and fear consumed every inch of my being.

Unable to process the surreal sight, I succumbed to the overwhelming terror, collapsing right outside the bathroom. Darkness engulfed me, and consciousness slipped away like sand through my fingers.

When I finally awoke, the morning sun was streaming through the windows, and the once daunting shadows had retreated. My family surrounded me, their faces etched with concern. Confused and still trembling, I recalled the harrowing events of the night and told them about the old lady. A serious silence settled over the room, broken by my aunt's words, "You haven't grown up a bit," followed by laughter from those around. I could see disbelief in everyone's eyes.

I stood up in anger and went straight to my room to get some rest. The sight of that lady from last night wouldn't leave me, and that very day, I decided to sleep in the same room where all the elders were sleeping. To avoid nature's call, I decided not to drink any liquid after sunset. Moved by my encounter with grandma (in my imagination for them), my uncle, for the time being, decided to remove the portrait of grandma from the hall.

Days later, we found my aunt in a similar state of shock, lying outside the same bathroom. On asking about what happened, she told in a trembling voice about the presence of a mysterious lady in a white sari lying on the hall sofa. She further explained that as she approached the sofa with curiosity and fear, taking small, hesitant steps, the figure which seemed to lay motionless suddenly stirred. In that chilling moment, my aunt's trembling voice resonated through the hall as she recounted her own terror. She told us it might be their long-lost mother.

In the aftermath of the chilling encounter with the mysterious lady in the white sari, an air of fear and anxiety enveloped the house. A thorough investigation was launched, and the decision was made – no one should venture alone at night. The spectre of fear had prompted the family to take precautionary measures against the unknown.

Neighbours, sensing the unease that spread throughout, generously offered their help. It was decided that a watchful pair, like 'chowkidars' in the night, would keep a vigilant eye on the basement, ensuring that the spectre of terror did not return to haunt our home. The community came together, fostering a sense of solidarity in the face of the mysterious and unknown.

A couple of nights later, when my father and uncle were on nocturnal patrols, armed with flashlights and an abundance of caution, they tiptoed through the dimly lit corridors, their senses heightened by the unseen presence that seemed to linger in the shadows. As the clock struck the ominous hour, a subtle creak resonated through the silence, like the soft whisper of an unseen spectre. The two men froze, their hearts pounding in their chests as they strained to pierce the shadows with their darting flashlights. There, in the hall below, a figure moved with ghostly grace.

"Who is there?" my father's voice reverberated through the stillness, cutting through the tension like a knife. The figure turned, revealing the silhouette of an old lady. The frailty of her form seemed compatible with the haunting aura that had gripped the household.

The warning shouts echoed through the house, jolting everyone awake. In a matter of seconds, the family converged in the hall, surrounding the mysterious figure. The old lady, bewildered and disoriented, blinked in the sudden flood of light.

Amid the tense atmosphere, a familiar voice cut through the suspense. "Wait a minute, isn't that Mrs. Sharma's grandma?" someone exclaimed. The realisation dawned on the gathered crowd, and the tension gave way to a collective sigh of relief.

It turned out that Mrs. Sharma's elderly grandmother was a sleepwalker, blissfully unaware of the nocturnal escapades that had sparked fear in the hearts of her neighbours. The connection between the houses through common stairs had inadvertently led her on a night's journey to the basement, turning her into an unwitting participant in the ghostly drama.

Laughter erupted from the gathered crowd as the truth unfolded. The atmosphere, once transformed into a scene of horror, turned into a humorous account. Mrs. Sharma, rushing forward to claim her sleepwalking grandma, wore a sheepish grin, apologising for the unintended late-night escapades.

So, the mystery that had shrouded the basement dissolved in the light of humour, leaving me with a tale to tell.

The memory of that fateful night from my summer holidays will forever stay in my heart, making me believe that I belong to this place and I have a story of a town connected with me. Remembering that night at my old Dadi's house still sends shivers down my spine.

4

Death Story

It was 7.30 am when Amar parked his bike in an open parking outside his office building. Everything around him was bright and sunny with a light cold breeze. Down the road, lush green trees exhilarated freshness, a nostalgic smell of Earth from the rain last night. It was a beautiful, nice day.

When Amar saw her for the very first time on the opposite side of the road, waiting at the bus stand, their eyes met for a brief moment.

"Did she really notice me ?"

With that thought, Amar walked into his office building with a smile on his face.

Inside, he still felt very happy about that eye meeting as he approached his desk, only to find out he was late for the morning meeting and everyone in the team was waiting for him in the conference room.

"Hello, Amar," a sarcastic voice came as he entered the room. "Welcome, welcome. Thanks for being so punctual and for your time."

"I am sorry, sir."

Amar took his seat next to his friend Prem as he shared some notes with him, and the meeting continued.

Amar and Prem met at the cafeteria for a cup of tea, where Prem told Amar that he should be giving more attention to his work as appraisals were round the corner, and getting late for meetings wouldn't do any good for him.

While heading home later that evening, Amar was thinking about his day in the office and the advice Prem had given him. He was near his society gate when suddenly a girl came in front of his motorbike, and they narrowly escaped a collision.

"Are you blind ?" Amar swallowed his incomplete words to the bottom of his throat as he asked, "I am so sorry, are you hurt ?"

A beautiful voice, after a brief pause: "I am fine. I should have seen it before crossing the road. I am so sorry,"

Amar, almost lost in thought, was stunned by the beautiful girl. Quickly gathering himself, he said, "It's ok."

As she walked past Amar, he kept looking at her.

He didn't believe what just happened. She is the same girl whose eyes held his gaze in the morning in the parking lot. What are the odds... he is surprised... and wanted another coincidence to meet her as he can't stop thinking about her all night.

The next morning, Amar and Prem were at the client's office. The day was hectic, involving meeting everyone at the client's office, listening to their feedback for the project, and sharing an important to -do list on priority as they completed their tasks for the day and headed to eat lunch around 4 PM in the nearby café.

They were sitting at the corner table at the cafe when Prem was explaining how good the day went at the client's location. Suddenly, Amar noticed a girl sitting a few tables away with fair pink skin, curly brown hair, and dark eyes — to his surprise, she was actually the same girl from the accident before.

He couldn't stop himself from reaching out to her. As Prem saw him walking past the tables and sitting in front of her, he intervened.

"I don't know why, but for some unknown reason, I had a sudden urge to come here and introduce myself to you," Amar said.

Monica raised her eyebrows questioningly, trying to remember him.

"Hi, I am Amar."

" Oh, hi - you. Hi, I am Monica," Monica said, remembering the yesterday's accident sequence.

"I am so sorry about yesterday."

"It's okay."

"This is the third time we are incidentally at the same place and seeing each other," Amar said.

"Three times," Monica said, surprised.

Amar explained to her how he saw her outside his office, the accident, and then here at the café right now. Startled by Amar, Monica noticed him for the first time. He is a cute, charming boy. They chit -chat about some things where she tells him about herself, that she is new to the city and lives near the east end of the city when Amar tells her that he lives nearby only, and they get lost in the conversation when suddenly Prem intervenes.

"Hello, Amar."

"Oh, I am sorry... Monica, this is my collegue Prem."

He joined in, and the three of them had some coffee and chips as the day set before bidding bye. Monica and Amar had exchanged their numbers.

The city witnessed a light rain shower that evening. Amar was heading home with all the lovely, playful thoughts about Monica in his mind. He is feeling more lively than ever in life in the past few months and thought what a beautiful place to live in as he noticed the city as looking at it for the first time.

Amar was lying in his bed thinking about Monica... how can someone be so pretty? Her mysterious dark eyes, her personality both alluring and captivating, her sharp physical features, she is truly a work of God, a beautiful girl inside out.

Suddenly, his cell phone beeps. (It's her.)

Monica: Hey, just wanted to say thanks for the evening. I really had a great time.

Amar (Blushing): Me too! You looked beautiful today.

Monica: Awwww. Thank you. You looked pretty cute yourself.

Amar: HAHA, Just cute? (wink) You had a really cute smile with charming dimples.

Monica (Impressed): Wowww, Thank you! That's such a sweet thing to say.

Amar: I am just telling it like it is. (wink)

Monica: I think you are going to be my first friend in the city:)

Amar, grabbing the opportunity: Certainly yes. How about we grab dinner this weekend if you are free?

Monica: Sounds great. Looking forward to it.

Amar: Me too. See you soon. Take care!!

Monica: Take care. Good night!!

Amar was out of this world after thinking about dinner with Monica.

He kept looking at the text conversation with Monica every few minutes on his phone.

He is getting excited and restless and just wanted to skip to the weekend at the dinner table. His heart skips a beat thinking about a dinner date with Monica.

The next day, Amar told Prem about the conversation with Monica over a cup of tea and asked him for some suggestions for the dinner date at the weekend. But opposite to his name, Prem didn't seem very interested.

Amar: Bro, I haven't thought in my wildest dreams that she will message me.

Prem: Who thinks about messaging a girl in their wildest dream? (Laughs loudly) I am getting myself a burger. Do you need anything?

Prem gets up from the table, giving a silly laugh to Amar.

By the next weekend, Amar made sure that he has completed all his work and handed it over to the client so that there is no scope of work on the weekend.

He has also finalised the place for the dinner with Monica.

As she walked straight towards me, I was looking at her. She looked beautiful... more beautiful than any other girl I had ever seen. The warm, inviting, and serene atmosphere added to her charisma. The decor was elegant with soft lighting and delicate fresh flowers. The seating was intimate, the atmosphere became more magical with her presence, creating a perfect ambience for a romantic and memorable night.

I stood up and greeted her, and for the first time, we hugged each other. I felt my heart skip a beat. She was delicate and beautiful. I was in the eye of a storm, the calm centre around which everything revolved.

She was like a rose in full bloom. Her smell made me lose count of the time as I was filled with joy.

"You looked stunningly beautiful."

"You look great too."

Both of us were smiling and blushing, making ourselves comfortable.

Suddenly, Monica's phone rang, and she told me that she is sorry but she had to leave as she had to take care of some urgent business. She apologised to me in a hurried manner, gave a kiss on my cheek, and left.

Amar, unable to understand what just happened, stood up with mixed feelings as he watched her leave. His heart sank a little, but he is excited and happy about the kiss, thinking about moving a step ahead in the relationship, ignoring her sudden disappearance from the dinner.

His night went by waiting for her message. Next morning, he is not feeling like himself and told Prem what happened last night. Listening to his story, Prem could not stop laughing and said, "Tera to kat gaya bhai," and started laughing again.

"But she kissed me," Prem said in a high pitch to counter his friend's laugh and not to feel bad about himself. Prem started laughing again as they both walked to their desks and resumed their work.

At around three in the afternoon, Amar got a call on his phone from Monica. She is apologising for yesterday, but Amar is in a bad mood and tries ignoring her over the phone, saying he is busy with work... unable to convince Amar, Monica said that she is outside his office and waiting for him downstairs.

Listening to this, Amar had a new wave of energy flowing through his body. He completely forgot about last night and rushed downstairs to meet her. The moment they met, they hugged, and Monica told Amar how sorry she is and that she is badly missing him from yesterday. Amar also told her how he spent his night waiting for her call and message. They both talked and talked, and before leaving, they both hugged each other and kissed passionately. It was the most tender thing I have ever touched. How can someone be so soft ? After a brief moment, they said goodbye, and Amar went back to the office.

Prem caught Amar Blushing and Smiling Entering the office and asked him what happened. Unable to hide his excitement, he told everything that had just happened with all his face red and shiny.

But Prem being Prem Sarcastically said, "There is something fishy about this girl she might be using you." Amar could not believe his ears, got irritated, and told Prem to get lost and stay away from him.

With Time Amar falls blindly in love with Monica. Every Once in a while, Monica disappeared suspiciously and ditched Amar on certain Occasions, and just before Amar could say something, she deceived Amar with her charm and innocence that Amar completely forgets about his anger and starts blooming in her love again.

She is happy. He is more than happy, and their love grows manifold with the passing time.

It was Friday night. Amar was in his alluring dream when he suddenly woke up with his phone ringing. It was 2 am, and an unknown number is flashing on the screen. Frightened, he picked up the phone, and all he could hear was someone sobbing on the phone. He could sense some wickedness in the situation.

"Monica, is it you ? Everything all right ?"

"Amar, please come and meet me. I am very scared. I am waiting for you outside your apartment. Please hurry up... " and the phone hangs up... "Beeeeepppp... "

Scared, Amar ran downstairs outside his apartment and was shocked to see Monica there in a grimy situation.

"What happened ? Why are you crying ? What are you doing here ?" Confused and frightened, Amar's head is filled with so many questions.

"I am really sorry. I really had a bad dream and I just wanted to meet you... " Tears run down Monica's eyes.

"It's okay, it's just a dream... come let's go inside. I will make you some tea."

"No, Amar, you are not understanding. It felt so real... " Monica, scared, hugs Amar tightly. "I do not want to lose you."

Amar kissed her forehead. "No, you are not going to lose me," and they stayed there for a few minutes before walking into the calm and breezy night outside Amar's apartment.

"Tell me what happened... What did you see ?" Amar asked.

"Amar, you are going to die... " Monica's holding Amar's hand in hers.

"Relax, Monica. Nobody is dying, it's just a dream."

"No, Amar, you are going to die, and I am just here to meet you for the last time... " Amar started to get uneasy with Monica's changing expressions, but holding himself, he said, "Baby, I am here only. Nobody is dying, you are just scared," interrupting Amar, Monica said, "Thank you, Amar. You have really made me understand what love is and why human life is worth living for. I will always be in debt to you for this."

Feeling scared, Amar tried to untangle his hand from Monica's and said, "Let's go back Monica. You are traumatised by the dream. Stay in my house, get some sleep, and you will feel better."

"There is no going back now, Amar. I just wanted you to know that I truly loved you, and I have never had the feeling of love before I met you... I will always remember you."

Mixed with fear and anger, Amar tried to untangle Monica's hand and pushed her as she was saying, "I just wanted you to know... " Suddenly, a loud banging... thud... sound came as Amar pushed Monica with all his strength and leaned backward before finding himself between the footpath and road... A speeding car hits him, and he falls some 20 metres away, taking his last few breaths...

Monica runs towards Amar with her head held down and with a mischievous smile with tears on her face... "I just wanted you to know, Amar, that I am Death on a vacation to Earth, and you have made this holiday surprisingly attractive... I will stay here for a while before leaving."

Yours truly,

Monica

5

Many Head Monster

"If by any chance holy water spills on the ground, the evil forces will rise from the pits of fire and destroy the holy city hidden for years."

It is said that many years ago, there was a fight between a 'Blue Warrior' and a treacherous Monster which lasted for a very long time until Mother Earth became infertile.

As the dark age expands, the warrior becomes weak and starts losing dominion.

Mustering all its power and force, with the last final swing of his sword, he managed to cut one of the heads of the "Many Head Monster" before vanishing into thin air.

Presently, the Earth is ruled by the Many Head Monster with the support from his 'Army of Hell.'

Everything that happens in and around the world, even in the remotest corner like a crab taking a volcanic bath at 'Nemo Point' or a mother feeding her child in the sub- Saharan region, does not go unnoticed by the 'Hell Army,' whose network runs deep into the Earth through 'canals of fire.'

But there is this one place which exists in the folklore of the common people, and the Hell Army cannot discover it yet. The place is hidden from the map of the world, and even the " Many-Headed Monster" is scared by the existence of that place.

This city, known as the 'Silver City,' is said to be the home of the 'Blue Warrior,' where he cut off the head of the Many -Headed Monster, and the spill of the blood marks the boundary of the spell that makes the city invisible to anything evil.

Spells and their Effects

It is believed that before vanishing into the air, the 'Blue Warrior' had cast a spell through which a pot of sacred holy water emerged in the centre of the silver city, and it is the only thing that can bring back the warrior and end the reigns of the Monster. But, "If by any chance or accident that holy water spills on the Earth, the city will be revealed to the Evil Hell Army, which will rise from the pits of fire and destroy the holy silver city hidden for years."

Ganesh, a young boy with big dreams, lost his mother when he was very small to the slavery of the

Hell Army and now lives in the capital city of the Many-Headed Monster with his father.

Their family, like many others, has also surrendered their faith to the will of Monster's Hell Army.

His father works as a cook in the kitchen, responsible for making food for the Monster's army, which helps them survive.

Growing old, Ganesh has always heard about the legend of the Blue Warrior and the invisible silver city. Seeing atrocities and crimes all around, he has made up his mind to discover the silver city and bring back the warrior to end the reigns of the Monster and kill him once and for all.

He will never forget the day he almost lost his father to the Hell Army just because he had forgotten to put some black pepper in the soup made for the army.

'BLOOD SOUP, ' a recipe originally invented by Ganesh's father, is the new favourite of the Hell Army. For that, he had been promoted to the 'head chef,' but in the process, he had lost his thumb from the right hand and the little finger from the left hand to the tasters of the Hell Army.

The main ingredient of the blood soup, which enhances its taste to heaven, is the tiny blood drop of the Blue Grasshopper, which is very rare, but Narayan always manages to get the next batch delivered before the previous one ends.

No one knows how Narayan operates or from where he gets the blood of a blue grasshopper, but he always delivers it on time and commands very high respect among people for the same.

Blue Grasshopper is a very rare sight to be seen ; only one in thousands have ever seen it. But on the day when Ganesh's father is to be prosecuted for the black pepper mistake, Narayan brought thousands of roasted grasshoppers for the Hell Army and saved Ganesh's father's life with seven fingers and a thumb. From that day, Ganesh started admiring Narayan and became his best friend.

With time, Ganesh also started helping his father in the kitchen. Whenever Narayan was in town, Ganesh spent most of his time with him and talked about his burning desire to kill the Monster.

As years passed, Ganesh mastered the art of cooking and, along with his friend Narayan, started exploring different places in search of the silver city.

On these quests, Ganesh did not find anything significant about the silver city but came back with assortments of different herbs and ingredients from the places he visited.

In his free time, he started experimenting with all the different ingredients he got. Stories of his delicious food started reaching the Many-headed monster himself.

One fine day, as Ganesh and his father were wrapping up their day in the kitchen, they were summoned by the Monster himself. Before they could think of anything, they found themselves standing in the courtyard of the Monster.

Ganesh's father became very fearful, negative thoughts surrounded his mind. He thought this would be the last day of their life. As he was dwelling in his thoughts and about to lose his mind, they heard things that nobody in the entire empire could believe.

Ganesh and his father were surprised to know that the Many -headed Monster had fallen in love with the daughter of his old ally and friend, the princess of the "LIZARDOUS EMPIRE."

The story in town is that the Monster had lost his heart at the first glimpse of the slick, shiny, and spearheaded tail of the LIZARDOUS princess.

As they stood in the haunting courtyard beneath the watchful eyes, the 'Many -headed monster' made its presence.

The heads atop its twisted necks were a nightmarish sight: some resembled venomous serpents, their fangs dripping with toxic venom, while others bore the features of ancient scholars with gnarled beards. His heads were crowned with jagged horns. Each head had its own distinct voice, and the cacophony of their simultaneous speech sent shivers down the spines of all who bore witness.

Monster, with his heavy voice, told them to prepare a feast for his special wedding day and a special soup to start the feast that no one has ever tasted before. They were given freehand to use any human, animal, or anything which can possibly be eaten for the menu or the soup.

After listening to the instructions, they were taken back to the kitchen, and one of the Monster's generals told them to complete the menu quickly. The wedding would be held in 11 days, and no mistakes would be entertained this time.

Listening to this, Ganesh and his father got scared because this time bad taste wouldn't be spared; death is imminent if anything goes wrong.

That evening, Ganesh met Narayan and told him about the Monster's wedding and his disappointment seeing him getting settled in life, "I want to kill that Monster, Narayan."

As they both discussed the wedding, the legend of the blue warrior also arose, and Ganesh insisted on finding the silver city before the Monster's marriage and bringing back the blue warrior to end the miseries of the Many-headed monster.

Seeing Ganesh's anger, Narayan told Ganesh that during all these years, he had been to the remotest part of the world, and from his personal experience and wisdom, he could only say that the myth of the blue warrior only exists in stories. Nobody is coming to save anybody; only you can save yourself. People's cowardliness is the strength of the Monster, and he sees this marriage as an opportunity to fight the Monster.

Listening to Narayan's words, Ganesh was shocked. Narayan told Ganesh that he had the white blood of the black sheep, the most deadly poison in the world, and he could use that in the wedding feast to kill the Monster.

Ganesh got feared and stunned hearing Narayan's plan but got convinced to end the Monster's life and avenge his mother, father, and all these people suffering from years and years of Monster barbarism.

The Feast Begins

Everyone is exhilarating in joy after eating the sumptuous feast cooked by Ganesh and his father. In such a joyful environment, the Many-headed monster kissed the lizardous princess, and they were bound in the beautiful relationship of marriage. But destiny had its ways. Their happiness didn't last long. Within an hour after the feast, everyone was dropped dead, including the Monster and his newly wed princess. Everyone was shocked to their core when Ganesh and Narayan revealed their plan and told everyone about the poisonous soup made from the white blood of the black sheep to end the reign of the Many-headed monster from the Earth. From that moment forward, they became the new warriors, and everyone lived happily ever after (**AT LEAST IN the STORY**).

THE END

6

The One Who Departs

We keep thinking about life in terms of a project, more like a 'science project,' and after successful completion, we finally think of living, where everything seems hunky -dory and we do not have to hustle and struggle. Until we realise new discoveries are always happening, and the deadlines are always pushed further.

Then, after a point, we started thinking of leaving the project unfinished and facing what may come our way, only to realise that we are the only subjects in this big experiment addicted to external stimulations.

I never had, in my short lifespan, thought about that. One day, life slipped out of my hands, and I was sitting above the world in the midst of white fairy clouds, thinking about life after losing it. An irony in itself.

Actually, that's human nature, 'to think about things that we lost once,' but I am human no more.

Since childhood, I have been the most lovable child in the family. My parents, brother, sister, my uncle, aunt, everyone, even in the extended family, used to like me a lot, and I think they still do.

Everything is very nice, warm, and cosy out here at my new abode above the clouds, and the best part is I can watch each and everything on Earth, just like a live broadcast, watching people change channels.

I am having a good time over here, and I am in no mood for rebirth again.

After living for so long and leaving my beloved body almost three years ago, I have realised things which never struck me, which I have never understood when I was alive... . "The one who departs is the one to experience loss."

It's always the way, but I lack to see it. It's all part of the game; the show never stops.

The day I was gone, everybody cried. Everybody mourned in their own way ; some declined food, some declined colour. Nobody wants to face the truth that I am gone ; nobody wants to say goodbye.

As the days passed, I was the only topic in the house ; I was in their dreams. Everybody remembers me. I was in, out, the centre of their thoughts.

I felt sad and sorry for them, but at the same time, a feeling of love crossed my heart, and I felt happy. There is always a contented smile on my face.

Father, mother, my siblings, my friends, everybody used to remember my presence. It's like I never left their space. While doing things and making decisions, they talk about my likes and dislikes and take action accordingly as I was always there.

As a cultural tradition, they offered and hosted a grand meal of my favourite food to the needy ones at the temple. They even organised a Puja for my well -being wherever I am. Do charity on my name and help the needy ones.

My mom and dad even keep my name as their passwords. I was everywhere after I was lost.

My room, books, clothes, toys, gifts, each and everything is very well taken care of; even my brother and sister are not allowed to keep my things.

My mother used to cry every single day, remembering me.

I feel the same for them. They are very cherished. The only thing is that I can see them, but they can't ; they have each other to share their emotions, but I have no one. A void is formed.

This has continued for almost a year, as cultural ritual practices do not allow them to celebrate festivals also. Then it's time for them to celebrate their first festival without me after a year. They all get emotional when my name was tossed up in some conversation, then they moved ahead, laughed, enjoyed, and celebrated the festival.

Now they also have a new family member, a cute little dog, whose care becomes utmost priority, something they look forward to.

Now with time, my mother also gets adjusted and moved on with life. Sometimes she remembers me and starts crying, but now tears are dry.

She has to be a strong lady for other kids to be taken care of.

My beloved things, my room, and property which my father has put on my name on my 15th birthday, are now being divided among others.

It's like a gap is being filled now for them, but I am still all alone up above, suffering for their love.

Now I have also stopped watching them as they only remember me on birth and death date just like any other normal ritual.

And today after three years, they have stopped taking my name. The dog has more importance than me in the house.

It is in my destiny to leave early so I have to suffer the most. The ones who left behind truly belonged to each other until they realised what I realised is the ultimate truth.

Now it's time for me to leave all this behind and get into this vicious circle of life and death to create some new memories, to gain some things, to lose somethings.

I will always cherish and miss my time over here, these more than comfortable warm clouds, the purer than pure environment. Maybe I will forget all these things and places, but I certainly think this is the harsh truth of life.

Come, Achieve, Let it go, and Leave peacefully.

A story by Meenakshi.

7

Jungle Adventure

The summer sun hung high in the sky, casting its warm rays down upon the lush green landscape of Uttarakhand. In the heart of this picturesque region, nestled amidst towering trees and winding paths, lay the quaint village of Maheshkhan. It was there, amidst the tranquillity of nature, that I and my childhood friends had decided to embark on a small vacation trip.

Gathered together on a pleasant sunny day, we met in our hometown Kashipur, excitement palpable in the air as we prepared for our adventure into the jungles of Mahesh Khan.

After a few hours of driving along the winding mountain roads, we found ourselves immersed in the breathtaking scenery, surrounded by towering peaks and lush forests. Laughter and jokes filled the air as we soaked in the beauty of our surroundings, enjoying every moment of our journey together.

As we approached the forest of Maheshkhan, where our booked guest house awaited us, we took a sharp right turn onto the forest road leading to our destination. Along the way, we noticed pine cones scattered across the road, creating a playful obstacle course. Raj, with his quick wit, suggested turning this into a game. Without much hesitation, we all joined in, clearing the pine cones from the road and transforming our journey into an impromptu adventure.

The Game

We imagined ourselves as members of an army troop, on a mission in the forest of Mahesh Khan. The pine cones scattered across the road seemed like hidden bombs, challenging us to navigate safely. Raj, always one for creativity, proposed a game where we had to clear the " bombs" without leaving the vehicle.

We convinced our friend Major Shah to slow down the car, and with determination, Raj and I swung open the rear doors and started collecting and throwing the pine cones away down the mountain to remove all the bombs from the road while our fourth friend Nitin, disinterested in the game, opted to doze off instead of joining in the excitement.

Clearing the road of pine cones felt like living out a childhood fantasy, as if we were conducting our very own military operation. It was a moment of pure exhilaration, blending imagination with the thrill of the present moment.

As we were caught up in our game, time slipped away like a passing breeze. Before we knew it, dusk was upon us, casting a soft glow over the landscape. We realised that we were nearing the guest house where we would be staying for the next two days, nestled deep within the jungle. The fading light added an air of mystery to our surroundings, heightening our anticipation for the adventures that awaited us in the heart of the wilderness.

When we finally arrived at the guest house, we were warmly welcomed by two house helpers who offered us a refreshing local drink made from 'rhododendron' flowers.

Settling into our accommodations, we quickly made ourselves comfortable.

As darkness descended outside, we gathered in the cosy hall, illuminated by the flickering flames of the fireplace. Sipping on our drinks, we relaxed and caught up with each other, reminiscing about our school days and sharing stories of the challenges we'd faced in our lives since then. It was a tranquil evening filled with laughter and joy, the perfect way to unwind after a day of adventure.

The guest house was arranged with rooms on either side of the central hall, which boasted old royal furniture including large sofas, tables, and ornate paintings. The hall was the heart of the guest house, with four doors leading to different areas: two to the rooms, one serving as the entrance, and another leading out to the backyard.

After enjoying a couple of drinks, we decided to step outside onto the back porch for a smoke. It was then that we noticed how dark it was in the jungle surrounding us. Strange noises echoed through the jungle, and we could hear the growls of unseen animals, sending shivers down our spines.

In case I missed telling you, when we arrived at the guest house, we noticed that the main property area was enclosed by gardens and surrounded by thick iron barbed wire from all directions. Curious about this, we asked the local boys who were helping us around the house. They explained that the fencing was for our own safety, as tigers and leopards were frequent visitors to these parts of the jungle. This revelation added an extra layer of caution to our stay, reminding us of the wild beauty and potential dangers of the surrounding wilderness.

As we relaxed on the back porch, illuminated only by a single bulb hanging in the corner, we found ourselves deep in conversation about our futures. Suddenly, we hear a loud voice - "I dare you, any of you, to go in the dark and touch the fence surrounding the property and come back."

Raj, always one for adventure, piped up with a daring challenge, stirring our egos and igniting our adventurous spirits. However, to his disappointment, all of us responded with a unanimous "No." Unhappy, Raj went back inside and picked a comfortable, cosy spot near the fire. As the night grew colder, I began to feel a slight headache creeping in. Deciding it was best to call it a night, I bid my friends farewell and headed off to bed without eating dinner, leaving the three of them behind to enjoy the rest of the night.

The next morning, I awoke at the tender hour of 5 o'clock, greeted by the sweet symphony of melodious bird songs. Casting a glance around the room, I observed my companions still lost in the embrace of deep slumber. Without disturbing their peaceful rest, I quietly retrieved my camera and tiptoed outside, eager to capture the enchanting beauty of the mountain morning unfolding before me.

Stepping outside the house at the break of dawn, I found myself entranced by the beauty of the morning. As I captured images of the glistening dew and the clear sky, a faint growling in the distance momentarily sent shivers down my spine. Yet, I reminded myself that the night had passed, and the morning held promises of new adventures.

Suddenly, my attention was diverted by the sight of a stunning Verditer flycatcher perched atop a nearby tree, enjoying its morning meal (A Tapeworm). Mesmerised, I began to approach the tree, eager to capture its beauty through my lens. However, a rustling in the bushes nearby caught my attention, stirring a sense of apprehension within me.

Putting aside my camera, I cautiously made my way towards the source of the noise, determined to confront my fears. As I neared the fence, I couldn't shake the feeling of being watched. With a steady resolve, I switched my camera to recording mode, prepared for any unexpected encounters.

Suddenly, a magnificent bluebird (Black headed Jay) emerged from the bushes, causing my heart to skip a beat. Yet, as I observed the bird's graceful movements, I felt a wave of calm wash over me. With newfound confidence, I continued to photograph the birds, revealing the vibrant colours of the morning light.

Lost in the beauty of the morning, I became aware of a presence nearby. Startled, I called out to my friends, but only silence greeted me in response. A bead of sweat trickled down my forehead as a sense of unease washed over me. Fearful that a predator lurked nearby, I hurriedly retreated indoors.

Upon entering, I discovered that my companions were still fast asleep. Despite my failed attempts to rouse them, I found solace in the safety of the guest house. With the morning still young, I decided to take advantage of the opportunity for some extra rest.

The day began to stir around eleven in the morning, finding us all eager and prepared for the adventures that awaited us. With sharp appetites, we decided to venture into the nearby small town of Bhowali for breakfast. Stepping outside, we couldn't resist capturing a few snapshots amidst the lush greenery of the jungle before setting off on our journey.

As we made our way towards the main road, our housekeeper handed us a list of items needed for dinner. With the list in hand, we continued on our path, surrounded by the tranquil beauty of the jungle. In just 20 minutes, we reached the road, and within the hour, we arrived in the quaint town of Bhowali. The journey itself was a delightful experience, filled with peace and serenity at every turn.

Upon our arrival in the town, we indulged in a hearty breakfast and took care of the necessary shopping for the day. It was during our interactions with the local shopkeeper that we learned about a nearby gem called Tagore Point, renowned for its breathtaking views. Intrigued, we decided to embark on the 3 -kilometre hike through the jungle to reach this scenic spot.

The trek proved to be quite an intense experience, with us traversing the winding paths of the jungle in solitude. Along the way, we encountered a majestic sambar deer, whose sudden appearance startled us as it darted past, disappearing into the depths of the forest below.

Being alone in the wilderness can be a daunting experience, as the mind plays tricks on you, conjuring up sights and sounds that heighten the senses. The sight of tiger claw marks etched into the bark of trees added an eerie element to our journey, reminding us of the untamed beauty and potential dangers lurking within the heart of the jungle.

Arriving at Tagore Point, we were greeted by an immensely beautiful vista spread out before us, stretching across verdant meadows. From this lofty perch, the entire town of Bhowali lay below, framed by the majestic mountains. The air was imbued with a refreshing crispness, invigorating our spirits.

In moments such as these, one feels truly alive, surrounded by the awe-inspiring beauty of nature. Lost in contemplation, I found myself pondering life's purpose and beyond, while my companions scattered to explore their own corners of peace.

As the cold winds began to sweep over the mountains, signalling the approaching dusk, we reluctantly decided to make our way back to the guest house.

As we journeyed along the jungle road back to the guest house, our peaceful drive was abruptly interrupted by the sudden appearance of a cow. Startled, we swerved to avoid a collision, narrowly averting disaster as the car teetered dangerously close to the edge of the gorge. Miraculously, Shah's skilled manoeuvring prevented catastrophe, bringing the vehicle safely back onto the road.

Confusion clouded our minds as we tried to make sense of what had just transpired. To our bewilderment, two local villagers approached us, expressing gratitude for saving the cow. Puzzled, we wondered how we could have been thanked for an accident we narrowly avoided.

Forgetting about the accident, lost in the rhythm of our journey, we sang and celebrated with mountain songs, our spirits lifted by the beauty of the surroundings. With carefree hearts, we continued on our way back to the stay house.

As we sat down for a late-night dinner, our housekeeper shared a startling revelation that left us frozen in disbelief.

"Bhaiya aap logon ki waja se humari Gaaye (Cow) bach gyi wrna Baagh(Leopard) use mar hi dalta." He explained that the noise from our car had inadvertently scared off a leopard, sparing their cow from becoming its prey. The realisation of our unintended role as saviours left us speechless, each of us exchanging nervous glances.

The thought of a leopard lurking nearby sent shivers down our spines, casting a shadow of fear over our minds. As we pondered the events of the evening, I couldn't shake the unsettling feeling that perhaps the creature I encountered earlier in the morning near the fence was indeed the very leopard we had unwittingly disturbed.

As we grappled with the startling revelation, a voice broke the silence: "Let's go outside, maybe we'll catch a glimpse of the leopard," exclaimed Raj. His suggestion divided us into two teams – Love and Nitin were eager to venture out, while Shah and I preferred to stay put.

In the midst of the tense atmosphere, the prospect of encountering a leopard stirred conflicting emotions within us. While some were drawn to the adventure, others, like Shah and myself, hesitated, wary of the potential dangers lurking in the darkness outside.

Despite our initial reluctance, Love and Nitin's persuasion eventually convinced Shah and me to venture outside in search of the leopard. With Shah at the wheel and me by his side, armed with a powerful torch, we set out into the darkness, hoping to catch a glimpse of the elusive predator.

As we drove along the shadowy roads, I grabbed my camera and began recording, eager to capture any sign of the leopard. Suddenly, a fleeting movement caught my eye as something darted across the road in front of us. In the dim light, all I could discern was the thick, unmistakable tail of the leopard disappearing into the night. Excitedly, Kush and I confirmed the sighting, while Nitin and Raj searched anxiously from the back seats.

Fear gripped us as we realised the predator was nearby and possibly hungry. Quickly, Shah reversed the car, heading back towards the safety of the guest house gate. Our hearts pounded in our chests as we witnessed the majestic creature in the open darkness.

Upon reviewing the video later that night, we were thrilled to see the leopard's tail captured on camera. Though Nitin and Raj, who were more eager to spot the cat, had missed the sighting, the memory of that encounter continues to send shivers down my spine to this day.

8

"Mind Your Own Business: Tale of Two Worlds"

Arjun grew up amidst the simple joys of village life. His days were filled with taking care of the family's cattle, navigating the winding trails that crisscrossed the hills, and listening to the ancient tales spun by the village elders around the communal fire. Life in Uttarakhand was a rhythm dictated by the seasons, a harmony of nature and community.

Arjun's family, like many in the village, relied on traditional practices for their livelihood. They cultivated terraced fields, growing crops that flourished in the mountainous terrain. In the evenings, the family gathered together in their small home, with dinner's warmth casting a glow on the old handmade walls adorned with local tapestries.

However, as Arjun entered his teenage years, the allure of the distant city caught his eye. Delhi, with its tales of grandeur and opportunity, captured his imagination. The boy who had grown up amidst the serene hills found himself drawn to the promise of something more, something beyond the familiar contours of village life.

Driven by a desire and a chance at a different future, Arjun left his village in Uttarakhand and embarked on a journey that would lead him to the bustling streets of Chandni Chowk. The transition from the tranquillity of the mountains to the frenetic energy of Old Delhi was both exhilarating and overwhelming.

In the narrow alleys of Chandni Chowk, Arjun navigated a world vastly different from the one he had known. The ancient structures, the complex blend of cultures, and the dynamic flow of life in Old Delhi were a stark departure from the simplicity of his village. Yet, amidst the chaos, Arjun discovered a sense of resilience that echoed the spirit of his mountainous roots.

As Arjun continued his journey, he delved deeper into the multifaceted layers of Old Delhi. He found work in a small shop, where the aroma of spices and the chatter of customers started becoming familiar companions in his urban adventure.

Amidst crowded lanes of Chandni Chowk his story unfolded like a tapestry of centuries-old stories. One sultry afternoon, the air was heavy with the fragrance of spices, and the symphony of voices created an intricate melody that echoed through the narrow alleys. The buildings, with their faded grandeur, stood as silent witnesses to the passage of time, bearing the imprints of a history that unlocked like layers of an ancient manuscript.

As Arjun navigated through the complex streets of Chandni Chowk, the colours of the bustling market enveloped him. The vibrant hues of saris and turbans mingled with the earthy tones of street vendors' stalls. The clamour of bargaining and the sizzling sounds of street food filled the air, creating a sensory kaleidoscope that defined the essence of Old Delhi.

In the midst of this organised chaos, his destination was the famous "Paranthe wali gali." As he strolled through the lively market, an unexpected disturbance disrupted the rhythm of the day – a chorus of shouts echoing through the narrow alleys. "Thief! Thief! Thief!" Intrigued, he turned his attention to four agitated individuals chasing a middle-aged man through the centuries-old streets.

Driven by a youthful vigour inherited from his mountain upbringing, he felt a surge of anger and determination towards the apparent wrongdoer. Without hesitation, he joined the chase, his legs carrying him through the crowd with agility. As minutes passed, he found himself the sole pursuer as the others either gave up or took different paths in the confusing maze of alleyways.

The alleged thief led him through a complex twisting lanes, each turn taking them deeper into the heart of the old city. Finally, far from the bustling crowd, he saw him panting, surrounded by a group of bewildered onlookers who had been drawn into the spectacle. As he approached, ready to confront the man and restore justice, the thief, who he had been following for some time, tired and stressed, spoke to the crowd, his voice reaching Arjun's ears.

In broken sentences, the man claimed that he had been pursued by a gang of robbers from the market who were attempting to steal his belongings. His eyes pleaded for understanding, and the crowd seemed torn between disbelief and sympathy. Stunned by this unexpected twist, Arjun found himself in a confused and difficult situation. Whose side should he take? Was the man before him a victim or a clever thief using a well-crafted story to escape the clutches of justice? As the man regained his breath and looked up, Arjun's eyes met his, and he raised a pointed finger towards the side of the road where Arjun was standing.

Suddenly, realisation struck Arjun's mind that he was still a stranger in this bustling city, far from the serene hills of his home. And unwittingly, he had pushed himself into a situation he barely understood. With newfound wisdom, he quietly slipped away, unnoticed by both the so-called thief/victim and the crowd surrounding him.

Back to his daily work routine at the spice shop, days went by quickly, and Arjun received his first salary at the end of the month.

One day, as Arjun was exploring the hidden corners of Chandni Chowk, he stumbled upon a forgotten courtyard adorned with Mughal-era arches. The courtyard, secluded from the bustling market, seemed frozen in time, a serene oasis amid the urban cacophony. Arjun noticed a man at the corner of the street wearing a red cap, a white shirt, and blue jeans. Familiarity struck Arjun, and he soon realised that it was the same man whom he had followed some time ago in a street chase.

As Arjun approached the man in the red cap, a surge of conflicting emotions overwhelmed him. The man turned, and recognition flashed in his eyes. It was indeed the same person he had chased through the labyrinthine alleys of Chandni Chowk. Arjun's curiosity mingled with a tinge of caution as he cautiously greeted the man.

The man, whose name turned out to be Ravi, thanked Arjun for his intervention that day. He explained that he had indeed been a victim of a gang of thieves, and Arjun's unexpected assistance had saved him from losing everything he owned. Gratitude warmed Ravi's eyes as he shared more about his life, his struggles in the city, and the challenges he faced.

As Arjun listened to Ravi's story, a bond formed between the two men, bridging the gap between their vastly different backgrounds. Ravi, originally from a small town in Uttar Pradesh, had also come to Delhi with dreams of a better life, but fate had dealt him a challenging hand. The streets had become his battlefield. Ravi told him about his job as a salesman and visiting different parts of the city on a daily basis.

In the days that followed, Arjun and Ravi together explored the bustling streets and discovered the tales hidden within the streets of Delhi. Arjun's connection with Ravi provided him with a new perspective on the city—its struggles, its secrets, and the unbeatable spirit of its people. As days turned into weeks, Ravi shared more of his struggles, and Arjun became a confidant. Ravi's dream of a better life seemed more achievable with Arjun by his side.

One day, after work, Ravi took Arjun to his small abode where he lived and offered him to stay overnight for dinner.

The warmth of Ravi's hospitality enveloped Arjun. The aroma of home-cooked food wafted through the air, and the flickering flame of a small lamp cast a soft glow over the room. Arjun couldn't help but feel flattered by Ravi's generosity, a stark contrast to the initial encounter in the narrow alleys of Chandni Chowk.

The evening unfolded with shared stories, laughter, and the clinking of utensils. Ravi's humble abode became a haven for Arjun, a place where the complexities of city life faded into the background. As they sat on the floor, savouring the simple meal, a newfound friendship blossomed between them.

The next day, as the sun bathed the city in a golden hue, Ravi introduced a proposition. "Arjun," he said with a warm smile, "why not stay with me permanently? We can share the rent and expenses. It'll be easier for both of us." Arjun, grateful for Ravi's kindness, considered the idea. The prospect of companionship and shared responsibilities appealed to him, and soon, he made the decision to move in with Ravi.

The transition to Ravi's home was smooth, and the two friends found solace in their shared space. Arjun continued working at the spice shop, and the days turned into a routine of work, exploration, and togetherness.

However, as life seemed to settle into a comfortable rhythm, fate took an unexpected turn. One day, as Arjun returned from the spice shop, he discovered a cold and desolate apartment. Confused and anxious, he searched for Ravi, only to realise that all his belongings were gone. It was as if Ravi had vanished into thin air, leaving behind a sense of betrayal and devastation.

Arjun's heart sank as the realisation dawned on him – the man he had come to trust had deceived him. The friendship they had built, the shared dreams of a better life in the city, all shattered in an instant. Arjun felt a mixture of anger, hurt, and a profound sense of loss. Ravi remained elusive in Arjun's mind, leaving behind a void that echoed with unanswered questions.

9

"Spiders and Scooters:
An Unlikely Friendship"

The morning sun cast a warm glow over the city as I embarked on my daily journey to the office. The crisp air hinted at the approaching winter, and I relished the idea of a slow ride on my old trusty scooter. Little did I know that this ordinary commute would turn into an extraordinary adventure, introducing me to an unlikely friend – a spider with six eyes and eight jointed legs.

As I navigated the bustling streets, the rhythmic hum of my scooter provided a soothing soundtrack to the urban symphony. The city was alive with the energy of another day beginning, and I couldn't help but feel a sense of anticipation. My mind was occupied with the usual thoughts – work responsibilities, deadlines, and the never-ending to-do list.

Little did I know that my routine ride was about to take a curious turn. As I approached a red traffic signal, my eyes wandered to the dashboard of my scooter, and there it was – a tiny creature with intricate features. Six eyes stared back at me, and eight legs clung to the surface. The spider was a marvel of nature, its thick black legs resembling tree barks, and its round, fluffy eyes exuding a sense of curiosity.

At first, I was taken aback, my initial reaction being a mix of surprise and fear. A spider on my dashboard was not a sight I encountered every day. As I contemplated stopping and removing the arachnid intruder, a pragmatic thought interrupted my impulse. What could I accomplish by halting my journey? I wasn't equipped to handle the spider with my bare hands, and my handkerchief was hardly a suitable tool for the task. Besides, I couldn't afford to be late for the office.

Decision made, I continued on my way, the spider inching closer to my hand. The traffic signal turned green, and I accelerated, leaving the curious spider undisturbed on my dashboard. The city sprawled before me, and the wind carried the scent of adventure as I ventured into the heart of the urban landscape.

As I rode through the underpasses near sector 18, the wind picked up speed, creating a potential hazard for my tiny companion. The last thing I wanted was for the spider to lose its grip and find itself airborne, possibly landing on me. The thought sent a shiver down my spine, and for a moment, I considered the risk of stopping again. But then, as if sensing my concern, the spider exhibited a surprising level of resourcefulness.

With deliberate movements, the spider repositioned itself towards the handle of the mirror, securing a safe spot away from the direct gusts of wind. It was a moment of silent understanding between a human and a creature of nature. We had embarked on an unexpected journey together, and it seemed we were both committed to seeing it through.

Exiting the underpass, the wind eased, and our unlikely companionship settled into a comfortable rhythm. I adjusted my speed, ensuring a smooth ride for both of us. It was at that moment that a peculiar thought crossed my mind – I felt like I was responsible for a small, delicate passenger in the front seat. The initial fear and discomfort gave way to a sense of responsibility and care.

The remainder of the journey unfolded like a unique collaboration between man and a spider. The cityscape transformed as we traversed through different neighbourhoods, each with its own character and charm. The spider remained a silent spectator, its multiple eyes taking in the sights, sounds, and smells of the urban landscape.

I couldn't help but marvel at the intricate details of our shared experience. The traffic lights changed from red to green, pedestrians crossed the streets, and other motorists went about their daily routines – all while my eight-legged companion clung to the mirror, unfazed by the bustling world around us.

As I approached my office, the realisation dawned that our time together was coming to an end. I felt a twinge of reluctance to part ways with my unexpected friend. It had become more than just a spider on my scooter; it was a reminder of the often-overlooked wonders of the natural world and the interconnectedness of all living beings.

Parking my scooter at the office entrance, I gave a nod of thanks to the spider passenger that had made my commute so extraordinary. It lingered for a moment on the handle of the mirror, as if acknowledging our shared journey. With a sense of gratitude and a newfound appreciation for the small wonders of life, I entered the office, ready to tackle the day's challenges.

Throughout the day, my mind would occasionally drift back to the morning's adventure. The spider, though small and seemingly insignificant, had left a lasting impression on me. It became a symbol of resilience, adaptability, and the unexpected beauty that can unfold in the midst of our daily routines.

In the following days, I couldn't help but keep an eye out for my arachnid friend during my commutes. While it never reappeared, the memory of our journey lingered, adding a touch of whimsy to the routine of my daily life. The city continued to buzz with activity, but

I found myself more attuned to the subtle wonders that often go unnoticed in the rush of the urban landscape.

Weeks passed, and the spider became a cherished memory, a story I would share with friends and family. It became a conversation starter, a testament to the unpredictable nature of life and the joy that can be found in the most unexpected places. The story of the spider on my scooter took on a life of its own, resonating with those who heard it and inspiring a sense of wonder in the seemingly mundane.

One evening, as I was leaving the office, I noticed a small group of colleagues gathered around my scooter, their eyes fixed on the handle of the mirror. To my surprise, there was another spider – not the same one, but a different spider making itself at home. It seemed the tale of the spider and the scooter had taken on a life of its own, attracting new eight-legged passengers.

The sight brought a smile to my face, and I couldn't help but share the story with my curious colleagues. The spider, once a source of fear and uncertainty, had become a symbol of unexpected connections and the beauty that can unfold when we embrace the world around us.

As the seasons changed and winter gave way to spring, the spiders on my scooter became a familiar presence. Every other day or two brought a new arachnid companion, and I welcomed them with open arms – or, more accurately, open handlebars. The once-unlikely friendship between spiders and scooters had become a quirky tradition, a reminder that life is full of surprises and that sometimes, the most remarkable stories unfold in the most ordinary moments.

And so, my daily commutes became a source of joy and anticipation, as I wondered which spider would join me on the ride each day. The spiders, in turn, seemed to adapt to their newfound mode of transportation, navigating the twists and turns of the urban landscape with ease. It became a symbiotic relationship, a testament to the resilience of nature and the harmonious coexistence of the smallest creatures with the human world.

And so, the tale of spiders and scooters continued to weave its way through the fabric of the city, a reminder that even in the midst of our busy lives, there is room for wonder, connection, and the unexpected friendships that can blossom in the most unlikely places. The once-fearful encounter with a spider on a scooter had evolved into a celebration of the beauty that surrounds us, inviting us to slow down, appreciate the small moments, and embrace the magic that can be found in the most ordinary of journeys.

10

Soda And Salt

In the heart of Delhi, where the bustling cityscape transforms with the arrival of winter, there lies a tale of cool breezes, misty mornings, and the warmth found in unexpected places.

As the days grow shorter and the sun takes on a gentler hue, our lives begin to sense the impending winter. The old banyan tree in the neighbourhood park, a silent spectator to the changing seasons, starts shedding its leaves. The children, bundled up in sweaters and scarves, gather beneath it, their breath visible in the crisp air as they exchange stories of the winter to come.

As winter sets in, enveloping our surroundings in a cocoon of cold, my wife and I find ourselves engaged in our routine evening conversations. We traverse over the common topics, the chatter of our respective workplaces and the gossip of the colony, delving into the topic of the arrival of Diwali and the sweet treats that come with it. The discussion takes the direction of exclusive cuisines for the festival, which in turn leads to a crucial question— what will grace our lunch table the next day, sustaining us through the rigours of our office and school?

After a brief exchange of thoughts, we settle on Rajma, the ever-comforting baked beans. Stirred from the warmth of my bed, I have to get out of my cosy warm place to cross the cold hallway to the kitchen. There, I set out to soak the beans in water, preparing them for the culinary symphony scheduled for the next morning.

A night of tranquil sleep embraces me. The hour at which my wife wakes up, the maestro of our kitchen, embarks on her morning routine, is a mystery. By the time I awake, she has orchestrated 80 percent of the household chores with her customary finesse. This is the first time that she is taking charge of the kitchen as our mother has left for her hometown in Uttarakhand.

Impressed by her culinary skill, I inquire about the progress of the Rajma.

"How's the Rajma cooking ?"

"Oh, the beans have metamorphosed into a mushy, unappealing state. I think we should get some fresh beans. They are all stale and rotten after cooking; they all get odourless and gooey," she replies.

A sense of disappointment washes over me, for I had envisioned a delightful lunch.

Coming on strong, my wife swiftly shifts her focus to yellow dal, assuring me of a comforting alternative. As I venture for a refreshing bath, my taste buds ready themselves for the savour of yellow dal.

As I ease into the soothing warmth of the tub on this chilly winter morning, a delightful cascade of tickles dances along my spine. The steam curls around me like a cosy embrace. As I lay there, the delicious anticipation of a hearty lunch begins to tango with my senses. Thoughts of yellow dal with warm jeera rice, and the enticing aroma of spices tantalise my imagination. The contrast of the cold winter outside and the blissful warmth within invokes a ticklish symphony of comfort, making the anticipation of a flavourful lunch a delectable daydream.

As I emerged from the warmth of my shower, I discovered a disconcerting reality — the dal, too, had succumbed to a peculiar fate. The vessel spread out a reddened, pungent concoction that defied all culinary logic. Bewilderment seized us as we scrutinised the raw lentils, searching for any signs of foul play.

A strange suspicion began to nestle in my mind. Was it our maid, who perhaps introduced a mysterious element into the vessels while washing the dishes? Maybe she had left some liquid soap in the vessel cover? Or did our gas supply harbour a hidden flaw? Undeterred, despite getting late for work, I resolved to uncover the truth behind our morning culinary drama.

My wife, recognising the culinary catastrophe, suggested we resort to our office canteens for lunch. Fuelled by a newfound determination, I delved deeper into the investigation. The vessel that once held the sumptuous taste of all the dishes now became the subject of my scrutiny.

Disassembling all its components and cleaning each part, I sought any signs of mischief. Finding none, I cleansed the vessel thoroughly and initiated the cooking process anew. Perhaps, I speculated, the fault can be laid in spices, so I started a renewed preparation of the lentils.

As the flames danced beneath the vessel, I put some dal in the vessel, poured some water, stirred it a bit and then I reached for the salt container. It was then that realisation struck like a bolt of lightning — it was not salt but soda! Shocked, I summoned my wife, questioning the contents of the container. She, with unwavering confidence, asserted that it was indeed salt, that she refilled that very morning.

In that very moment, a revelation dawned upon me — it wasn't the handiwork of a mischievous maid or spoiled beans; rather, the matriarch of our household, taking charge of the kitchen, she had replaced our entire culinary system with soda, and she took pride in her unconventional feat.

It seemed like a period of adjustment was in order for her after all.

The subsequent events after a comedic and chaotic mishap unfolded with a certain surrealism.

The vessel, now cleansed and ready for a fresh start, embraced the lentils once more. With measured precision, I added the spices, ensuring a careful balance of flavours. The flames beneath the vessel danced in a synchronised rhythm, casting a warm glow on the kitchen. My wife, observing this culinary renaissance, expressed a mix of curiosity and amusement.

As the aroma of cooking lentils filled the air, a sense of anticipation enveloped the kitchen. I carefully approached the salt container, this time scrutinising its contents with heightened awareness. The familiar white crystals and tangy pungent taste reassured me — it was indeed salt, dispelling any lingering doubts about soda infiltrating our culinary domain.

The lentils simmered to perfection, embracing the spices in a harmonious blend. The vessel, once tainted by the trials of the day, emerged flavoursome once again.

With shared laughter, the confusion, and the eventual triumph painted a vivid picture of the unpredictability that often accompanies everyday life.

As I savoured the carefully crafted lentils in my lunch break, I couldn't help but appreciate the humour woven into the fabric of our existence. In the days that followed, the tale of the soda mishap became a cherished anecdote, shared with our friends and family.

11

Khajjiar Trip

It was the start of winter when my friends and I made a plan to visit Himachal Pradesh for a short trip over the weekend.

The trip was going very well and full of fun and joy. We visited Khajjiar, also known as the mini Switzerland of India.

Little did we know that things were going to take an unexpected turn. Starting from the next day, while chatting with our driver whom we hired from Delhi, we got to know that this was his first car trip. He had recently learned to drive, and it was his first visit to the mountains. We all got scared at this thought: how could Sumit be so irresponsible to hire such an amateur driver for such a trip full of dangerous mountain roads ?

Settling this in mind, we decided that one of us should always keep an eye on the driver while he was driving.

That day, after breakfast, we decided to go paragliding. It was a straight climb up the hill where the takeoff spot was, and at the time, I weighed around 100 kgs. At first, it was a task in itself to climb that mountain. Somehow, I climbed up, and looking around was an amazing experience. Our pilots and trainers were already up there, ready with their equipment and kit. They told us all the basic dos and don'ts and asked us to sign a form, stating that if some mishap happens, it should be our sole responsibility, not theirs. Listening to this, a grumbling fear took over me. I was sitting on a big rock, watching people go one by one into the air. It was exciting and fearful at the same time seeing them fly.

When my turn came, there were four pilots, but each of them refused to go with me, seeing my big build and hearing them talk like, "You will go, you will go." I lost all my excitement, and fear took over me. I asked them what the problem was, and they told me that the wind was very slow, and I had too much weight. Without wind, we would straight fall into the abyss of this hill.

A lucrative fee for the ride convinced one of them to go with me.

They put all the gears and parachute around me, and we were prepared for takeoff.

Those of you who do not have a paragliding experience, let me tell you: it's like running towards the edge of the cliff with a heavy parachute behind you, and you have to run really fast to get that up in the air before your runway ends; otherwise, you won't be writing or reading this.

So I am all set with my pilot gear and parachute, standing on the runway when suddenly everything goes into pin -drop silence. It seems like suddenly we are in a vacuum; the air stops flowing, and I look towards my guide. Our eyes meet, and he says, "It's alright. As soon as the winds start flowing, we will fly," but his looks in his eyes defy his words. I get more scared, almost giving up on this experience when suddenly a flag, which they use to see the wind flow, starts waving.

We all take a long breath, a sigh of relief, and as we are good to go, we head down the slope towards the edge of the cliff.

My pilot tells me to start running, and he is tied up to me. He tells me to increase the pace as we have to lift the parachute up, but mid-run, he stops me abruptly, and we almost fall. I get up in anger and ask him what happened. He tells me that the wind has stopped once again, and we collect our parachute. Standing at the start point again, it's almost 15-20 minutes, and all of my friends by that time, I guess, have already reached the landing site.

I am so scared and fearful inside; if something happens again, I am going to die. I am almost on the verge of crying when fast winds start blowing, and my pilot says, "This is our chance," and we rush in full pace towards the edge of the cliff. When we jump, my heart is in my mouth. Instead of going up in the air, as soon as mine and my pilot's weight is on the parachute, it goes down. I see death between those beautiful pine and deodar trees down in the valley.

But as soon as I open my eyes, we are in the air, steady and slow. A joy of happiness and amazement, a feeling I cannot describe, takes over me. I start crying, seeing that mesmerising view from a different perspective towards this world.

As I am grasping this feeling, he tells me to hold the grip tightly as we are going on a roller coaster ride.

He swings the parachute to the left and then to the right, tilting it a bit. I feel like I slipped from my seat a bit. I get really scared and ask him what he is doing. He tells me, "This is the real deal; enjoy it." I say no, I don't want it, just keep it straight. I almost scream at him in anger and fear, and then plead with him to land it safely as quickly as possible as I am really scared.

After a few more minutes of diving into the air, we land safely, and it's an awesome feeling. But a fear in my heart already tells me never to do it again, at least not with that much weight. The area where our landing point was is in the middle of the apple orchard. A beautiful sight. We had some apples, had our lunch while eating. The owner of the restaurant tells us to visit 'Pohlani' Devi Temple ; it's 15 km from here, and the sunset there is the best you see in Himachal. On top of that, you can see Kailash Parvat (Mt. Kailash) there at the back of the Mata temple. It's a 2-3 km trek above the mountain top, and it's at the end of the road; after that, it's all Air Force area.

Excited by the description of the place, we decided to visit right after our food. We instructed our, so to say, never -experienced driver to take the car there. The road to the temple parking is full of dangerous turns, steep slopes, and narrow mountain patches. We were all feeling sleepy after the food when suddenly I saw our driver driving very recklessly on the road, speeding over the turns and ignoring the speed limit and the warning signs ahead. I told him to slow down, woke everyone up, and we all cautiously reached the temple parking with the driver, from where we had to trek to the peak.

At the foothill was a big gate leading to the trek to the temple. It was a beautiful sight, giving heartfelt pleasure to the eyes.

The way ahead seemed exciting, a small trail disappearing into the jungle with big, dense trees on both sides of the trail.

As we moved ahead on the trail into the jungle, we were mesmerised. The cold from the green, big deodar trees engulfed us. We were enjoying the cold mountain trek, moving ahead slowly and steadily. Nature never fails to disappoint us; as we passed the sharp bend in front of us, it opened up into large, lush green beautiful meadows, and the temple was in sight from there.

Amidst the beautiful meadows, there were 2-3 benches placed exactly where they should be to enjoy nature and sit after a long trek to talk to your inner self. As we approached, Vivek pushed me jokingly, and in that moment, I lost my balance and started rolling downhill. For a moment, we all thought I would drop dead into the deodar jungle, but luckily I stopped after a few rolls. Vivek apologised for this mishap but at the same time made fun of my weight.

After clicking some pictures, sharing jokes, and bantering, we moved ahead and reached the top of the temple.

There, we offered our prayers to the deity and sat in silence to experience the magic happening within ourselves. Then, we took a look around, only to be mesmerised by the majestic Himalayas standing tall, larger than life, and in between, we could see Mount Kailash, the abode of Lord Shiva.

I could feel the happiness and calmness within myself. We sat there and had Maggi from the only shop nearby. As the sun started to set just in front of the goddess deity, leaving the last rays, it seemed like the sun itself was offering its prayers to the goddess.

I can say it was the best sunset I have ever seen in my life ; it was magical. The clouds changing colour with the temperature of the sun, you name it, the colour on your palette, and it's there. It was something I had never seen before. I made a beautiful time -lapse of the sunset, contented and happy. By that time, we were the only people out there, and the boy who is closing its only shop at top.

We started our journey down the hill when that boy told us to go down quickly as there will be dark in the forest, and you are only seeing light here because you are on the top of the mountain. It's better to go down quickly because mountain jungles hold power beyond this realm.

Saying that, he moved quickly, and within minutes, he was out of our sight.

Tired from the day, we started the downward trek as quickly as possible, but we didn't catch up with the boy as we crossed the meadow and entered the jungle. Only then we realised what that boy was talking about; it was pitch black out there, the trail barely visible, and we had to put on our phones' flashing lights to see the path.

As we walked and walked and walked, fear started engulfing us, as no one wanted to move on. At the last spot, we started hearing noises, scared and feared. We don't remember when we got split ; Vivek and Tarun were out of our sight, and me, Prakansh and Sumit were left behind.

I was tired, as my body started getting fatigued because of the tiring day.

Suddenly, we felt like something is moving on with us. I told them that I heard footsteps from the jungle as if leaves were crumpled by the foot. I am scared; they told me to move fast. "It's in your mind," but soon after, they also feel like something is moving besides them.

Scared to death, Sumit, jammed due to fear of being unable to move, he started reciting Hanuman Chalisa.

We moved in closer to Sumit, rubbed his hand and face, washed his face with water, and then only he came back to his senses. Slowly but almost running, we were holding each other's hand and moving down, screaming our friends' names, but there was no response from them. Again, we heard the breaking of twigs and movement of foot as we stopped. The sound also stopped as we started moving. The sound also started moving as if it was following our rhythm and at that very moment, I lost my head and started running madly downhill, leaving my friends behind. I don't know how much time has passed, but as I reached the parking, I was shocked seeing that everyone was there and was waiting for me for an hour. I screamed out of shock and told them everything that happened in the jungle, and they told me that they were moving, and I was last in the trail. After some time, I lost from their sight; they waited for me for 15-20 minutes, but I didn't come, so they thought that they should go down and bring some help.

In a few minutes, the locals were there, and one of them told us that in the night, sometimes a lost soul gets onto the people, but they are harmless; they just want some company as they live alone in the forest. But there is this one incident when a tourist is lost last year not to be found again. Listening to this, I got fainted, only to awake in my hotel room later.

12

The Snoring Wife

Long ago, before people began flocking to cities in search of their livelihoods, there lived a young couple in a small picturesque village in Uttar Pradesh. The village was a haven of natural beauty, surrounded by lush green fields and serene calm jungle. Muniram and his wife lived a simple yet fulfilling life in this close-knit community.

Their days were woven with the threads of tradition and simplicity. Away from the complexities of modern urban life, instead of succumbing to the allure of city lights and the demands of contemporary employment like many others in the village, Muniram decided to open a small jewellery shop in the village market to take care of his family financially, and his wife took care of all the household chores. They embraced the tranquillity of their rural abode.

In this village, where time seemed to move at its own unhurried pace, one crisp winter night, Muniram was stirred from his sweet slumber sleep with a sense of unease prickling at the edges of his consciousness.

As Muniram lay there in the darkness of the night, the loud rhythmic symphony of his wife's snoring filled the room. Unable to ignore the disquiet that crept over him, he gently nudged her awake. "Is everything okay?" he inquired, concern etched in his voice. Through the fog of sleep, she mumbled in a drowsy affirmation, "Yes, yes," and with that, the melody of snoring gradually subsided. Reassured by her response, with the calmness of the night, Muniram also fell asleep.

Again, one night, Muniram found himself bothered by the loud snoring of his wife. He woke up feeling irritated and, with a gentle shake, tried to get her to stop snoring. However, this routine continued, and over time, the snoring seemed to grow louder and more persistent. One chilly winter night, the snoring reached an unusually loud level, disturbing Muniram's sleep. Despite his attempts to wake his wife, she remained unaware. In his half-asleep state, Muniram repeatedly asked her to stop snoring and even shook her gently, but she responded with sleepy, blurry mumbles. Frustrated and unable to find rest, Muniram decided to step outside.

As he stepped outside, Muniram noticed that the dark night was slowly turning into a bright dawn. He felt a bit restless and thought he had some time before the day officially began. So, he made a quick decision to take a walk through the peaceful village. The air was cool, and Muniram strolled along the quiet streets, doing his usual activities earlier than usual. This unplanned walk turned out to be a nice escape from the annoying snoring, giving Muniram a chance to enjoy the calmness of the village.

For several nights, Muniram found himself troubled by the ever-increasing volume of his wife's snoring. This routine persisted, and as time went by, the snoring only seemed to get louder.

One night, unable to sleep, Muniram tried waking his wife as usual, but she remained in a deep sleep, responding with blurry, half-asleep murmurs. Frustration built up, over an hour passed by, Muniram unable to return to sleep got irritated, he decided to escape the confines of his home and take a walk through the village.

Hurrying outside, Muniram, fuelled by slight anger and frustration, passed through the village. Along the way, he noticed a house brightly lit up, indicating a recent marriage celebration ; a smile passed through his face remembering all the delicacies from the evening before. Continuing towards the riverside, as darkness enveloped him, a sense of unease crept in. Despite his growing fear, Muniram pressed on, quickening his pace. He knew the way ahead; after passing this jungle dark patch and some barren plots and ongoing construction work, he knew that beyond the next bend, the familiar sight of village houses would emerge, providing a welcome relief from the unsettling darkness.

With determination pulsating through his veins, Muniram hastened his steps as he ventured into the dark, uncertain patch. Within mere seconds, his eyes discerned the silhouette of a woman adorned in a vibrant red suit, her bangles and jewellery glinting in the dimness. A wave of surprise washed over Muniram at the unexpected sight of someone dressed so elegantly at this late hour. Despite the curiosity, ignoring the woman, he maintained his course and focused on his own path.

As the woman drew nearer, a chill ran down Muniram's spine. Before he could fully process the situation, the unexpected encounter took a sinister turn. The woman, without warning, confronted Muniram, delivering 2-3 resounding slaps to his face. Startled and bewildered, Muniram, now frightened, was faced with an aggressive demand: "surrender all your money and the chain around your neck."

Terrified, Muniram pleaded for mercy, but his pleas fell on deaf ears. The woman, displaying a menacing demeanour, kicked him forcefully, causing Muniram to collapse on the roadside. In the midst of this vulnerable position, Muniram spotted a sharp stone nearby. The menacing woman continued to hurl abuse, warning him of dire consequences if he didn't hand over the items quickly.

Summoning every ounce of strength and courage, Muniram gathered himself, rising from the ground. In a swift and desperate move, he seized the sharp stone and, with precision, struck the woman below her mouth on the chin. The night erupted into chaos as she let out a piercing scream, collapsing on the ground.

As Muniram stumbled away from the fallen woman, a chilling sense of fear gripped him. Panic surged through his veins as he sprinted through the darkness, the echoes of the woman's haunting screams still lingering in the air. Suddenly, a menacing figure with long, dishevelled black hair and yellow teeth emerged from the nearby bushes and started chasing him with wild determination. The night seemed to stretch endlessly before Muniram, when the threatening words of the man echoed, "You will not get away, Muniram; the night is long, and you will be hunted. HAHAHAHA."

The maniacal laughter reverberated through the still night, intensifying Muniram's terror. A desperate urgency fuelled his steps as he bolted towards the comforting glow of distant village houses. However, his heart sank as he spotted another unexpected threat – a young boy, seemingly innocent, but with an unsettling aura, approaching from the front. The realisation hit Muniram: he was caught between two bad forces, a dire situation closing in from both sides.

In this intense panic, Muniram's mind raced, and in a split of a second, he made a decision and took off from the familiar path. It was an unexplored route, a third option that had never crossed his mind in the serenity of his village life. The village, now eerily silent, held its breath ; Muniram's unconscious decision led him into the bleak expanse of barren land. His breaths came in ragged gasps as he stumbled upon a large pile of sand, with a tractor trawler stationed nearby, surrounded by heaps of bricks. In pain and fear, Muniram, without pausing to consider, sought refuge beneath the trawler, burying himself in the shadows.

Dark silence enveloped the scene, broken only by the distant hum of the night. Muniram, terrified to his core, hiding beneath the trawler not to be seen, started waiting. As the seconds stretched into minutes, and with no sign of anyone, he cautiously peeked over the edge of the trawler. The eerie stillness of the night greeted him, and in the dim light, he checked the time – 3:25 am. Regret took over his mind, and he thought how stupid he is to get out of the house in such a hurry without looking at the clock.

A rustle of stones and twigs nearby shattered the stillness of the night, sending shivers down Muniram's spine. He peeked to find the source of the sound, his mind racing with thoughts of the gang that had threatened him earlier might have located him. Fear constricted his chest as he began to pray fervently, closing his eyes in a desperate plea for divine intervention. The suspense intensified as the darkness played tricks on his senses, heightening the tension of the moment.

The weight of exhaustion and the accumulated stress from the preceding nights pressed heavily on Muniram. In the midst of this turmoil, time blurred, and he lost track of when he passed out in fear.

When Muniram woke up the next morning, the sun was shining bright, and it was almost 10 o'clock. He stepped out from beneath the trawler and realised that he had slept really well. The workers were busy with their construction work, and Muniram couldn't believe how comfortable his accidental nap had been.

With a chuckle, he passed the workers, thinking about the strange adventure he'd had in the middle of the night.

Later, when he told his wife about the whole thing, she burst out laughing. "Well, Muniram," she said, still giggling, " Maybe a midnight adventure is the secret to a good night's sleep. Next time you're bothered by snoring, just consider it a cue for an exciting nighttime adventure!"

In the end, Muniram couldn't help but laugh along.

13

Summer by the Kosi

In the quiet town of Uttarakhand, the sun cast its gentle rays upon Rajat, who had returned to the embrace of his hometown after years of navigating the bustling city life. The streets, once familiar, now whispered tales of forgotten days, and the nearby Kosi River allured him like an old friend. With nothing much to do and without any of his childhood friends in town, one fine morning with a basket of sandwiches, Rajat decided to embark on a journey through the old memories of his childhood.

His motorcycle, a faithful companion, hummed with the promise of adventure as Rajat navigated the winding roads. The jungle, dense, quiet, and mysterious, with Rajat on his motorcycle on the path, tempted him with tales of unexplored villages and secret stories. As the engine's melody filled the air, Rajat found himself lost in contemplation, revisiting the echoes of a bygone era.

The road through the jungle, once walked with the laughter of childhood friends, now unfolded before him in solitude. A whiff of nostalgia accompanied each turn, and the dense forest held stories untold. As the motorcycle manoeuvred through the lush green patches of the jungle grass, Rajat's mind became a canvas painted with images of school days and wild encounters.

Fifteen minutes into the journey, the forest enveloped him, casting a spell of enchantment. Memories of childhood surged like a river, and he recalled the days when their school buses were stopped in deference to a majestic tiger crossing the path. The memory, once a source of excitement, now sent a shiver down his spine. Fear got stuck in his mind, and he started to feel that something from the jungle was keeping an eye on him.

The jungle road, a serpentine path through the heart of nature, seemed to stretch into infinity. An unsettling stillness gripped the air, broken only by the rhythmic beat of his motorcycle's engine. Rajat, now alone on the winding trail, felt the weight of the forest's gaze, as if the ancient trees themselves were watching his journey through time.

The silence was eventually interrupted by a rustling in the nearby bushes. Rajat's senses heightened as the motorcycle continued its journey. The rider, wary of the unseen, was met with the realisation that no other soul had crossed his path for quite some time. A strange and frightening solitude settled over the jungle, amplifying the sense of isolation.

The forest, with its dense canopy and concealed mysteries, played tricks on his senses. Rustling bushes hinted at an unseen creature. Rajat, caught in a web of anticipation, navigated through the dirt patch with caution. Just as anxiety reached its zenith, two old mountain ladies emerged from the nearby bushes, their presence a revelation that lightened the fearful atmosphere for Rajat.

The weathered faces of the mountain ladies, adorned with genuine smiles, offered a stark contrast to the fear that had gripped Rajat's heart. Their silent acknowledgement, a shared moment of warmth, left Rajat questioning the nature of the smiles—were they friendly or tinged with a hint of sarcasm, considering his solitary journey into the heart of the jungle?

Lost in these thoughts, Rajat's mind drifted to his old dear friend named Amit, who always accompanied Rajat on these adventurous explorations when they were in school. Childhood memories once shared had become distant as adulthood with responsibilities pushed everyone into different paths. The realisation struck him that he should have called Amit and told him about his trip to the town. The nostalgia that lingered in the air could bridge the gap between the present and the cherished past.

As the motorcycle wound through the last hairpin bend, the Kosi River unfurled before Rajat, a silver ribbon of clouds weaving through the clear blue sky. The distant memories of carefree days by the river rushed back. As Rajat parked his motorcycle, eager to jump into the flowing waters that had witnessed the tales of his past, the transition from the dense jungle to the open landscape of the riverbank was marked by a profound sense of anticipation.

Guided by the echoes of childhood laughter, Rajat approached the water's edge. A large rock in the middle of the flowing water invited him to sit, and Rajat surrendered to its silent call. The river, timeless and steadfast, seemed to welcome him back with open arms. Seated on the rock, Rajat found solace in the river's gentle murmur. Nature, in all its glory, became a sanctuary, and the symphony of flowing water and rustling leaves drowned out the distant echoes of the city.

The sun, now ascending towards its peak, cast a warm glow on Rajat, who, for a moment, became one with the tranquillity that surrounded him.

The river, a silent storyteller, carried Rajat through the currents of time. Memories intertwined with the gentle flow, and Rajat's heart swelled with gratitude for the simplicity of the moment. The motorcycle, now a silent observer, stood sentinel on the riverbank, a testament to the journey that had led him back to this sacred place.

As the sun reached its peak, casting an unrelenting glow, Rajat decided to cross the river. On the other side, a sprawling tree promised shade and a cool respite from the harsh midday sun. The motorcycle hummed to life once again, carrying its rider towards the river's embrace.

The crossing, marked by a causeway dry in the summer heat, provided a moment of reflection. Rajat, now on the opposite bank, gazed back at the vast expanse of river that separated him from the past. The journey, both physical and metaphorical, continued with the promise of a shaded sanctuary beneath the welcoming branches of the sprawling tree.

Under the tree's leafy canopy, Rajat surrendered to the lull of the afternoon. The river's melody, accompanied by the rustling leaves, created a symphony of nature that cradled him in a peaceful siesta. Time, momentarily suspended, allowed Rajat to drift into a dreamlike state, where the boundary between reality and imagination was blurred.

Yet, in the realm of dreams, a distant scream shattered the tranquillity. Jolted awake, Rajat found himself between sleep and wakefulness. The scream, a haunting echo, reverberated through the riverbanks, beckoning him to follow its source.

Compelled by an innate sense of responsibility, Rajat traced the riverbank for nearly 500 metres.

There, amidst the ebb and flow of the water, his vision unfolded— he saw an ethereal figure in distress. A village girl with a large chaff stack atop her head struggled in the middle of the river. Propelled by a surge of concern, Rajat rushed to her aid.

The scene, reminiscent of a fable, became a tableau of shared destiny. Bhawna's leg, injured by the river's unforgiving stones, looked up with a mixture of vulnerability and gratitude. Rajat, understanding the gravity of the situation, relieved her of the cumbersome burden and assessed the wound.

The connection between them, born out of the river's fateful intervention, deepened. Bhawna, caught in a moment of vulnerability, found solace in the stranger's compassion. Rajat, a silent guardian on the riverbank, became a protagonist in a story of chance encounters and shared trials.

With the chaff stack removed, Bhawna's injured leg became the focal point. Rajat, with a gentle touch, washed away the dirt and tended to the wound. The river, bearing witness to the unfolding drama, whispered secrets of fate and connection.

Rajat offered his shoulder as she, unable to move, crumbled with pain. He helped her move out to the riverside. As Bhawna bent forward to hold Rajat and put her arm around Rajat's neck, her leg slipped on the stone and Rajat, in a fluke movement, held her by the waist to prevent her from falling. At that moment, their eyes met, and a connection was made, frozen in the movement and mesmerised by Bhawna's beauty, a cold shiver of current flowed down Rajat's body.

As Bhawna's pain was soothed by the river's cool touch and kneading by Rajat, the two found themselves sitting by the water's edge, a strong bond forged in the crucible of an unexpected encounter. Rajat, drawn to Bhawna's simplicity and resilience, began to unravel the layers of his story.

The afternoon unfolded in a cascade of shared stories and laughter. Bhawna, a handful of village tales, painted vivid pictures of life beyond the jungle's embrace. Rajat, captivated by her sincerity, found himself opening up in return. The riverbank, by their side, witnessed the exchange of dreams, fears, and the silent yearnings of two souls destined to cross paths.

Rajat, lost in the rhythm of Bhawna's voice, became enchanted by the harmony of their connection. The sprawling tree, under which their destinies intertwined, cast a dappled shade over them. The sandwiches from the forgotten basket became a communal feast, consumed amidst laughter and the timeless melody of the river.

The sun, now descending from its zenith, cast a warm glow on the riverbank. Shadows danced in rhythmic tandem with the river's flow, and the two figures, seated side by side, became silhouettes against the canvas of the evening sky. Rajat, momentarily forgetting the passage of time, marvelled at the serendipity that had brought Bhawna into his orbit.

As the day waned, Bhawna, mindful of family expectations and the encroaching dusk, reluctantly expressed her need to depart. Rajat, torn between the desire to linger in the magic of the moment and the inevitability of parting, watched her silhouette disappear into the fading light.

A promise lingered in the air—a promise to meet again, a promise that resonated with the timeless flow of the river. Rajat, left alone on the riverbank, became a silent witness to the symphony of nature and human connection. The sprawling tree, their shared nature, stood as a silent guardian of the ephemeral encounter that had graced its roots.

Reality blurred with dreams as Rajat woke up to the screeching sounds of the jungle babblers fighting over Rajat's backpack for sandwiches. Shocked, lost of his senses, now alone, succumbed to the river's lullaby and the rustling leaves. Rajat woke up from his false awakening to a dreamscape where Bhawna's laughter echoed through the corridors of his mind.

The sandwiches, forgotten in the wake of a romantic encounter, became a sandy feast for the winged raiders.

Awakening to the babblers' antics, Rajat, now fully conscious, gazed at his watch. The hands pointed to 3 PM—a moment frozen in time, a testament to the slow pace of life by the river. Rajat, no longer just a visitor but a partaker in the river's tales, walked along the bank, washing his face in the cool, refreshing water.

Thoughts of Bhawna lingered, as a sweet residue of the day's serendipity. The backpack, now bereft of its contents, became a metaphor for the transient nature of material possessions. Rajat, with a renewed sense of gratitude and love, retraced his steps along the riverbank.

As the journey continued, the jungle, with its dense foliage and hidden mysteries, enveloped him once more. The motorcycle, patiently waiting on the riverbank, rumbled to life. The winding roads, now a familiar companion, guided Rajat back through the heart of the jungle.

The journey, both physical and spiritual, became a reflection—a bridge between the past and the present. The jungle, the river, and the memories woven into the fabric of Uttarakhand created a tapestry that stretched across time. Rajat returned home with a heart brimming with gratitude.

Uttarakhand, with its timeless charm, had given him a day of rediscovery—a day where the Kosi River became more than a tributary. It became a channel for stories, a witness to connections forged on a beautiful summer's day. The jungle, the river, and the lovely encounter with Bhawna became chapters in Rajat's ongoing journey through the landscape of memory and emotion.

14

Mr. Pant, and His Memorable Nickname

It was the story of a time when my folks thought it's best to shift me to another school to ensure that I had the best shot at a bright future.

They weren't quite content with how things were going at my current school. Little did I realise then, they were simply nudging me to squeeze out that extra percent in my studies and result.

Like any other hurdle, the admission process wasn't a walk in the park. I had to go through an exam, and let's just say I did okay, nothing extraordinary. So my parents did the rest of the bit, they really went all out, pulling strings and making requests left and right, just to secure me a spot in the esteemed INTERNATIONAL PUBLIC SCHOOL.

Just when I was all set to dive into my first day at the new school, fate had a different plan. A day before, I was diagnosed with jaundice, which meant I had to put the excitement on hold. A whole month slipped by as I battled the illness. When I finally returned, it was smack in the middle of the yearly unit tests. Thankfully, after some heartfelt requests and explaining my condition, they let me off the hook, sparing me from the test frenzy.

While everyone else was caught up in the whirlwind of tests, my only mission was to catch up on all the lessons I'd missed across all subjects.

On my third day, I met our English teacher. He was a lean, not-too-thin middle-aged man who carried himself like a British soldier. His voice had this commanding tone, making every sentence sound like he was issuing orders.

You see, as many of you may already know, and perhaps some of the younger ones are experiencing it firsthand, students have a way of sizing up their teachers and giving them nicknames based on their quirks.

As I settled into the rhythm of the new school, my friends and I couldn't help but notice something peculiar about our English teacher – he was always running late for class. Naturally, we decided to do a bit of sleuthing to uncover the reason behind his perpetual tardiness.

So, we took it upon ourselves to keep a close watch on the teacher's movements. Whenever he left the classroom or the staff room, we trailed behind, curious to unravel the mystery. It didn't take long for us to notice a pattern – he'd wander down the corridors or linger in the school garden before eventually making his way to class. After some serious pondering, we realised the truth: our poor teacher was simply confused about the layout of the school buildings and couldn't remember which class was where.

One fine day, just when we were anticipating a blissful free period since our maths teacher was absent, and we were eagerly looking forward to a game session, Mr. Pant barged into our classroom out of the blue. To our dismay, he declared an impromptu English test. Our hearts plummeted as we reluctantly put away our hopes of a fun game period and reluctantly opened our English textbooks to begin the test.

Amidst the quiet concentration of the test, Mrs. Sinha, from the administration department, unexpectedly burst into our classroom. She questioned Mr. Pant about why he hadn't conducted the scheduled test for class 9A, mentioning their rowdiness in the corridor. Every eye in the room turned to Mr. Pant, awaiting his response. With a hearty laugh, he admitted his mistake, "Oh, I am so sorry, Mrs. Sinha. I got into the wrong classroom."

Apologising to Mrs. Sinha for the confusion and the disruption, he then bid us farewell, promising to reschedule the test for the following week.

As he left, we couldn't help but conclude that Mr. Pant had a knack for forgetting things.

As the seasons shifted, our half-yearly exams swiftly passed, and the results were finally unveiled. Eagerly awaiting Mr. Pant's arrival to hand out our report cards, we found ourselves growing increasingly impatient as time stretched on without a sign of him. Glancing out the window, I caught sight of Mr. Pant making his way across the corridor, with some of my classmates lingering at the classroom door. In a moment of jest, I called out, looking at Mr. Pant's appearance, "Come inside, thin Leaf is flying in the corridor."

As Mr. Pant stepped into the room, we greeted him with a cheery "Good Morning, Sir," to which he responded, "Ah yes, you're calling me 'Leaf' now."

We all controlled our giggles, but Munish couldn't contain his laughter and ended up receiving a sharp slap on the cheek for his indiscretion.

I remained silent, knowing I was the culprit who had shouted the nickname. As our results were handed out, I was pleased to find that I had performed well in English, earning myself a distinction.

As the years rolled by, Mr. Pant became known to future generations as "Thin Leaf," his quirky nickname lingering on in school lore.

15

The Marble Girl

1

Rani was sitting on the front porch of her small house, staring at the sunset. Her best friend, Arjun, approached her slowly and sat down beside her. They both remained quiet for a few moments, watching the sun go down.

Finally, Rani broke the silence with moist eyes and unshed tears. "Arjun, I don't know how to say goodbye," her voice choked with emotion.

"Rani, what about us? Our dreams that we have seen together. Our future. We can make it work if you don't have to go," Arjun's eyes pleading to hers.

"I'm going to miss you, Arjun," Rani replied softly. "I wish things were different. I have to leave now."

Arjun looked down at his hands, feeling a lump forming in his throat, his voice cracking. "But it's going to be so hard without you here. You're my best friend. I don't know what I'm going to do without you."

Rani put her hand on top of his, giving it a gentle squeeze. "I'll still be your best friend, Arjun," she said reassuringly. "And who knows? Maybe one day we'll be together again."

Arjun looked up at her, his eyes filling with tears. "I love you, Rani. I always will."

2

As I headed back home, I stopped by a local sweet shop and picked up some Balushahi, Rani's favourite sweet since childhood. I knew she would be delighted to have it, and it will make her day a little brighter.

Father: "Here, take these Balushahi, but remember to eat them one at a time."

Daughter: "Thank you, father. You are the best."

Mother: "You're spoiling her with your love, giving her sweets like that. You should be scolding her for skipping school and playing marbles all day."

Father: (chuckles) "Let her have some fun. She's just a child. Besides, playing marbles might help her develop some strategic thinking skills."

Daughter: (smiling) "See, father understands me."

Mother: (rolling her eyes) "Oh, please. She can't keep skipping school and playing games all day. All you're doing is encouraging her to become a street urchin."

Father: (laughing) "Don't worry, dear. She will be fine."

Mother: (sighing) "I give up. You two are too much."

Despite the constant financial struggles, Rani's father was a remarkable man, always giving his family the best he could offer. Every day, he woke up early and moved all around the village to do his job as a postman. He never once complained about his meagre living conditions, and instead focused on making the most of what they had. His unwavering love and dedication to his family were truly admirable, and Rani couldn't help but feel a deep sense of gratitude and respect towards her father.

3

Rani's love for marbles started when she was just a little girl. She would watch the boys play from her window and long to join them. Her affection for marbles was indescribable. Rani's school bag contained more marbles than books. One day, she mustered up the courage to approach them and asked if she could join in, and that's how she met Arjun. In between the games, they became close friends.

Rani had always dreamt of becoming an international marble player and building a life for herself out there in the world, but she never shared her dream with anyone. Her mother grew tense seeing her spending hours practising and perfecting her shots, often neglecting other things and scolding her.

Arjun: "Hey Rani, I have something to show you. Do you want to come with me ?"

Rani: "Sure, where are we going ?"

Arjun: "Just follow me."

Arjun leads Rani to a field near the village pond, where he has set up a marble game.

Rani: "Wow, this is amazing! I've never seen so many marbles in one place."

Arjun: "I know, right? I just wanted to show you my collection."

Rani: "Teach me? You are the best ?"

Arjun: "No, not at all. You are better than me."

As Arjun starts showing her some marble tricks, their hands brush against each other, sending shivers down Rani's spine.

Arjun: "You're a natural champion, Rani. You're picking this up so quickly."

Rani: "All thanks to you, Arjun."

They both share some laughs together.

Arjun: "You know, I really enjoy spending time with you."

Rani: (Blushing) "I feel the same way."

Arjun: "I was wondering if you'd like to go on a date with me sometime? Maybe we could play marbles again ?"

Rani: (smiling) "That sounds like a lot of fun. I'd love to."

They continue playing marbles and talking, enjoying each other's company as the sun sets behind them, their hearts beating as one.

4

It seems that after a while, we are not able to achieve the life we envisioned for ourselves. We feel that the life we are living is a lie ; we know where we need to be in life going ahead. However, by that time, a lot of time has passed, and life seems to have slipped away behind us.

Rani's father had suffered from a heart attack.

Rani's world had turned upside down ever since her father's heart attack. Her mind was clouded with worry and the weight of the responsibilities that had fallen on her young shoulders. She longed to escape to the world of marbles, to play with her friends, and to forget her troubles, but she couldn't. She was constantly preoccupied with her father's health and the financial burden that had been placed on their family.

Rani: "How are you feeling, father ?"

Father: "I am fine, beta."

Rani: "Do you need anything ?"

Father: "No. I am just worried about you and mother."

Rani: "Don't worry, father. I have applied for a marble tournament in the city. They will provide me with a free scholarship if I clear the entrance round. I will take care of you and mother, I promise, father."

There is silence in the whole room. Rani's father's face turns pale with anger and depression listening to Rani's words. After a brief moment of silence, mother walks into the room, and Rani's father shatters the silence and her dreams.

रानी की माँ: "इसके हाथ पीले करने का वक्त आगया है।" (It's Time to get her married)

5

As the days went by, Rani found herself growing more and more distant from Arjun. She missed him terribly. Every night, as she lay in bed, Rani's mind would wander to the days when she and Arjun would play marbles together, lost in their own little world. She longed for those carefree days, but it seemed like a distant dream.

As much as she loved her family, Rani couldn't help but feel a sense of bitterness creeping in. Why did she have to shoulder all this responsibility? Why couldn't she be free to live her own life, to pursue her own dreams? If she were born as a boy, would marriage be the solution to every problem ? Would she be a burden to the family then? But as these thoughts swirled around in her mind, she knew deep down that she could never abandon her family.

A message beeps on Arjun's mobile -

"I want to meet you, Arjun."

Rani was sitting on the front porch of her small house, staring at the sunset. Her best friend, Arjun, approached her slowly and sat down beside her. They both remained quiet for a few moments, watching the sun go down.

Finally, Rani broke the silence with moist eyes and unshed tears. "Arjun, I don't know how to say goodbye," her voice choked with emotion.

"Rani, what about us? Our dreams that we have seen together. Our future. We can make it work if you don't have to go," Arjun's eyes pleading to hers.

"I'm going to miss you, Arjun," Rani replied softly. "I wish things were different. I have to leave now."

Arjun looked down at his hands, feeling a lump forming in his throat, his voice cracking. "But it's going to be so hard without you here. You're my best friend. I don't know what I'm going to do without you."

Rani put her hand on top of his, giving it a gentle squeeze. "I'll still be your best friend, Arjun," she said reassuringly. "And who knows? Maybe one day we'll be together again."

Arjun looked up at her, his eyes filling with tears. "I love you, Rani. I always will."

Young girls like Rani from rural villages in India often face numerous challenges when it comes to pursuing their dreams. Financial struggles within their families often force them to prioritise survival over their aspirations. For Rani, the young girl from a remote village, her love for marbles and ambition to make something of herself were constantly in conflict with her family's financial reality. Her father's health only added to her burden, leaving her with the responsibility of taking care of him and putting her dreams on hold. Such struggles are not unique to Rani; countless young girls in similar situations are often forced to sacrifice their dreams due to circumstances beyond their control.

16

Holi Adventures With Father

It was that time of year again, when the air was changing and the vibrant festival of Holi was just around the corner. I was sitting with my father and some relatives, gathered together as he began to share tales from his childhood in our hometown of Ramnagar.

It was around that time when Ramnagar was a quiet little town nestled amidst the mountains of Uttarakhand.

My father and all his brothers and sisters lived in a place called Bhawani Ganj in Ramnagar. It was an important spot for labourers and wood traders because a lot of wood cutting and loading took place in and around the nearby jungles.

Around the time of Holi, they all became charged with excitement, especially because of the discounted alcohol at the local wine shop. Being far from home and working as labourers, this brought them immense joy. They felt like doing all sorts of adventurous, nonsensical, and sometimes even ridiculous things, as if this was their only chance to truly live.

On the morning of Holi, after playing with colours within the family, there's a tradition to visit and greet other relatives and neighbours to celebrate the festival together.

This year, my cousin Amit came all the way from Delhi to celebrate Holi with us. He didn't know much about the Holi celebrations in our beautiful town of Ramnagar.

Let me tell you a bit about our town: there are two river streams flowing through the town, and the main road goes over them, connecting one part of the town to the other. After wishing everyone a happy Holi and playing with colours around the house, we decided to visit the other part of town where our uncle lived.

Remembering the frightening stories of past Holi celebrations, we left the house fully prepared. We made sure to give clear instructions to Amit bhaiya about the river patch where all the rowdy labourers gathered to celebrate Holi in unconventional ways. The key was to stick to our own path, avoid talking to anyone, and if someone came too close, run and don't get caught. Despite being the eldest sibling, Amit bhaiya simply nodded as if the instructions were nothing out of the ordinary.

We stepped out of our home and were greeted by streets painted in various vibrant shades imaginable. Before we knew it, we were nearing the river. As we approached, we could see the remnants of last night's "Holika Dahan" ritual, with the woods still smouldering. People were dancing, play-fighting, and enjoying themselves. From a safe distance, we could sense that the locally made discounted alcohol had taken control of them. We knew we needed to pass through quickly to avoid any trouble.

We were walking behind my father and uncle when I noticed a few people from the other side had spotted us. Sensing trouble, I whispered to Amit bhaiya that we should walk faster. Suddenly, my uncle got hit with a water balloon on his back, and he yelled for us to run or else this Holi would be unforgettable for all the wrong reasons. In the chaos, we all started running. Looking back, I saw those people chasing us.

Amit bhaiya seemed to be enjoying all the thrill, responding to them by throwing water balloons back. It was all fun until one big water balloon hit him on the face, causing him to lose balance and fall. We all stopped and tried to rescue him from the rowdy labourers, but it was too late. In just a few minutes, they had stripped him of his kurta, covered him in cow dung, and tossed him into a small stream of water beside the road, where the other labourers were revelling.

When we reached the spot, the labourers surrounded us with excitement, eyeing us as if we were their prey. But my father's quick thinking caught them off guard. He burst into loud laughter, and we followed suit. He wished all the labourers a "Happy Holi" and offered them sweets meant for our relatives. He even handed them 100 rupees for booze. The labourers, shocked, surprised, and suddenly happy, pulled Amit bhaiya back and began apologising.

As we left the scene and continued walking, we couldn't help but laugh at Amit bhaiya, walking around the city bare-chested like a tough guy. He was clearly upset, walking ahead of us and saying that this wasn't the way to celebrate a festival.

My father chuckled and reminded him that we had warned him not to get caught. We laughed together and made our way to our other uncle's place, where Amit bhaiya got a new shirt and became the subject of many jokes about his Holi adventure.

Years passed, and now Amit bhaiya himself became a father. But to this day, he still remembers the terror of that Holi and has never visited our town during the festival since then. 😄

Poem's

1

Childhood Romance

———— ◆◆ ————

I was a little scared of love,

seeing you every time gave me butterflies in my stomach.

The aim of the day was to look and say 'hi.'

On a bonus day, we exchanged books for a day.

At times it was difficult as teachers looked for prey.

The day you were upset, I wished I could stay.

I sat beside you for Saturday activities.

I always wanted to sneak in with you.

With rare finger touches, my feelings jumped too.

All of this in my heart, little scared to say,

Those were beautiful days, before our childhood parted ways.

- Neil

2

Bottle on the Beach

I remember vividly as I hold the drink,

Weather is on the brink, with waves getting shrink.

It was early in the day, beer was our play.

The beach is nice and the fish king -sized.

Friends are near with nothing to fear.

As the day gets tipsy, I feel like a gypsy.

As the sun is dawning, I was yawning.

The day got sloshed, and the picture got clocked.

- Neil

3

Belief

If you believe in life,

you will always feel alive.

If you believe in hard work,

luck will always be by your side.

No matter what situation arises,

you will always emerge big and wise.

When all the cards are falling around you,

have faith and stand true.

If you walk without fear,

the path will be victorious, bad luck will disappear.

People will forget whatever you've done,

the path will be there,

someone else has to rerun.

- Neil

4

Busy People All Around

As I head into the town, I see busy people all around.

Being busy is nothing new ; people now have screens
to which they glue.

Faces illuminated with the digital debut,

spines are down with hearts full of ego,

lost in the sea of likes and follows.

Everything aligns in the concrete jungle,

with chaos arriving in the digital bundle.

From work to worship, everything is brand new.

In this digital age, even gods have to debut.

Amidst this chaos, some moments breakthrough,

connections are made, emotions shine through.

- Neil

5

Tale of A Neglected Flower

A few days ago, I found you crashed.

Your petals were vibrant, giving life a fresh dash.

I clicked some pictures and abandoned you like trash,

you were lying on my table, waiting to get refreshed.

I went out of town to get some rest,

only to find out you'd already taken your rest.

In my absence, you silently sighed,

as your vibrant colours began to hide.

I have learned a lesson, and it's clear,

cherish and protect what you hold dear.

Life is like fleeting grace,

nurture and preserve it in every place.

- Neil

6

Feeling Of You

Looking forward to the day,

I know you will stay.

We will talk and eat together,

in this warmth and lovely weather.

The depth in your eyes is a sight to behold,

your presence in my arms makes my nerves hold.

The melodies surround us,

have no fear,

keep the trust,

these moments are dear.

Time is flying, like a storm,

making you, my dear, more adorned.

Keep it in your heart,

it's your time to leave,

enduring love story that once we weave.

- Neil

7

I Will Be Brand New

The days were breaking like an old rotten trunk,

everyone around was sulking like a drum.

Life is nothing but the same old rhythm,

follow corporate culture to boost your ego vulture.

Wake up to the alarm with sleep getting harmed,

the showman hypnotised the family ; they keep thinking lazy.

No one wants to care, just keep running the fair,

one day I will leap through and will be brand new.

- Neil

8

January Love

January love, a chapter unfolds,

young hearts fabricating stories in the cold.

Small fights, sparks fly in the air,

yet resolutions bind, a promise to care.

Dew -kissed mornings, pristine white,

covering paths of each small fight.

In between classes, passing notes full of passion,

romance whispers in concealed fashion.

Young lovers traversing, new depths,

steaminess rising, as desire begets.

Exploring new affection, this beautiful fire,

January love, our hearts aspire.

Deeper we delve, hand in glove,

love gets intense, embracing itself in snow.

- Neil

9

Melodies of Time

Retreating monsoon's hues of blue,

life was going through and fro.

Golden glee invokes memories of you,

in that moment, I was touched by you.

With September's cold air, I was writing to you,

every turning page embracing you.

Alone in the garden under night's dew,

moon shining with silver soft hue.

Charming birds held a love affair,

warmth of those days was lovingly rare.

Weathers keep changing with the golden glee,

my love for you is a timeless melody.

- Neil

10

Mistaken Life

Life full of fear,

Job has to be dear,

No time to spare,

Flying like aimless spear,

Money encircles your mind,

More is always your rhyme,

The day you were born,

Expectations tag along,

Life has passed beyond,

You keep running on,

Now when you know life,

Days are grey and quiet,

Life is no race,

Hold on to a beautiful mistake.

- Neil

11

October Love

Mornings don't feel so lazy now,

winters don't feel so cold now,

school does not feel so boring now,

friendships do not seem to care now.

October brings back the smell of love,

when we share lunch in the woods.

All of this will go down the lane,

I will be a writer and you will be a name.

One day a gust of wind will blow,

name will be recited and love will follow.

- A poem by Neil

12

Old Man's Tale

Story behind a story which I tell you,

time lies beyond the tale I tell you.

Old man's dream never came true,

he has fallen prey to the silence of few.

Preaching vultures within family came through,

his only strength the love that stands true.

On the banks of time from where he is passing through,

there lies an honour for a man so true.

Life is fair to only a few,

be the old man when hard times surround you.

- A poem by Neil

13

From One to Eleven

When I was one, laughter and joy begun.

When I was two, my experiences grew.

When I was three, life is jubilee.

When I was four, everything is sour.

When I was five, I became naive.

When I was six, my spirit started to mix.

When I was seven, I yearned for eleven.

When I was eight, life opened its gate.

When I was nine, my heart bathed in moonshine.

When I was ten, I needed yen.

Now that I am eleven, I want to be seven.

- Neil

14

When I First Saw You

❈

The age was tender, the heart was blue,

the meadows were green and the sky had a hue.

When I first saw you,

I was scared and the impatient you,

I know the love deep down was true,

when I first saw you.

You taught me how to handle my brew (coffee),

with all the cold days that went far from you,

I know the love deep down was true,

when I first saw you, when I first saw you.

- Neil

15

Whispers of the Night

As I am going to sleep through the night,

with moonlight by my side,

a clock hanging beside, whispering in the quiet night,

when a butterfly caught my sight,

sliding into the shadow of light.

The time is ticking and the fly is kicking,

my sleep is gone, lost in the world of its own.

A loud horn is blown and it's almost dawn,

car is passing by, with city life screaming hi.

My eye left my sight searching for the golden flight ,

but it is gone and it's my time to move on.

- Neil

In the Womb

In Mommy's belly, comfortable and warm,

I'm brewing like a perfect storm.

Parents plan and grandparents dream,

celebrations are coming in full steam.

The talk of my places and toys galore,

I'm here, unseen, but they adore me.

In father's dreams, I take a peek,

Mommy describing her world, oh so sweet.

Tiny clothes and nursery themes,

 imagining me in adorable schemes.

Mom's cravings, oh, the foodie spree,

I'm in for a taste of a grand entry.

Grandma knits, Grandpa beams,

a family woven in hopeful dreams,

far from the West my aunt flies high,

a twinkle in her expectant eye.

They plan a party, full of cheer,

for the day I finally appear.

But in this belly, snug and round,

I hear the joy, the giggles around.

I'll join the fun in a while,

bask in their love, graceful style.

A tale untold, a bundle unseen,

but in their hearts, I'm already king/queen.

- A poem by Neil

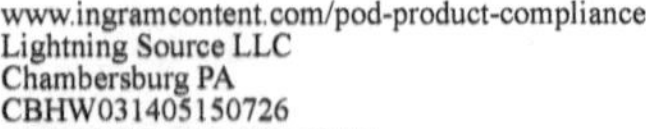